GRIEVER

An American Monkey King in China

Illinois State University/Fiction Collective Series

Curtis White, Series Editor

Also available in the series

PLANE GEOMETRY AND OTHER AFFAIRS OF THE HEART

by R.M. Berry

WHEN THINGS GET BACK TO NORMAL

by Constance Pierce

Griever

AN AMERICAN MONKEY KING IN CHINA

❦ A NOVEL BY
GERALD VIZENOR

ILLINOIS STATE UNIVERSITY
NORMAL
FICTION COLLECTIVE
NEW YORK · BOULDER

This publication is the 1986 winner of the Illinois State
University /Fiction Collective Award, jointly sponsored by
the Illinois State University Fine Arts Festival and the Fiction
Collective.

Published by Illinois State University/Fiction Collective with
assistance from Illinois State University Foundation and the
National Endowment for the Arts; the support of the
Publications Center, University of Colorado, Boulder; and the
cooperation of Brooklyn College and Teachers & Writers
Collaborative.

Forward all inquiries to: Fiction Collective, c/o Department
of English, Brooklyn College, Brooklyn. N.Y. 11210.

The characters in this novel arise from the author's imagination; any resemblance to actual persons is purely
coincidental.

Library of Congress Cataloging in Publication Data

Vizenor, Gerald Robert.
  Griever: An American Monkey King in China.

I. Title.
PS3572.I9G7 1987   813.'54   1987–11860
ISBN: 0-932-51109-0
ISBN: 0-932-51110-4 (pbk.)

Typeset by Fisher Composition, Inc.
Manufactured in the United States of America.
Designed by Abe Lerner.

DEDICATED TO

MIXEDBLOODS
AND
COMPASSIONATE TRICKSTERS

g

*Writing is a search for the meaning that writing itself
violently expels. At the end of the search meaning
evaporates and reveals to us a reality that literally is
meaningless. . . . The word is a disincarnation of the
world in search of its meaning; and an incarnation: a
destruction of meaning, a return to the body.*

OCTAVIO PAZ
*The Monkey
Grammarian*

g

*Chinese drama is largely nonrepresentational or
nonmimetic: its main purpose is expression of
emotion and thought, rather than representation or
imitation of life. In other words, it does not seek to
create an illusion of reality, but rather seeks to
express human experience in terms of imaginary
characters and situations.*

JAMES J. Y. LIU
*Essentials of Chinese
Literary Art*

CONTENTS

PART 1 Xiazhi: Summer Solstice   11

BOUND FEET   13

HOLOSEXUAL CLOWN   19

JADE RABBIT   27

PEKING NIGHTINGALE   31

MATTEO RICCI   34

GRIEVER MEDITATION   48

FREE THE GARLIC   52

MUTE PIGEON   56

PART 2 Dashu: Great Heat   63

PANIC HOLES   65

STONE SHAMAN   72

BLACK OPAL   79

PEACH EMPEROR   88

PART 3   Bailu: White Dew   107

       VICTORIA PARK   109

       OPERA COMIQUE   124

       SWEET PICCOLOS   132

       EXECUTION CARAVAN   138

PART 4   Quifen: Autumn Equinox   159

       OBO ISLAND   161

       DUCK WEBS   178

       OUTDOOR MOVIES   192

       FORBIDDEN CITIES   201

       BLUE BONES   212

       BLUE CHICKEN   227

       ULTRALIGHT ESCAPE   231

EPILOGUE   236

PART 1

XIAZHI: SUMMER SOLSTICE

The way in which daily speech was filled with expressions and metaphors taken from the stage clearly attested to the hold that theater had over life. A Chinese sociologist has most convincingly described how the Chinese tend to look at human behavior in terms of role-playing and to consider themselves somewhat as actors playing their own existence.

SIMON LEYS
Chinese Shadows

The ordinary Chinese man on the street wears simple, uncomely clothes . . . he appears worn down, polished thin by the labor of centuries, his very body as smooth as a hammer grip.

PABLO NERUDA
Passions and Impressions

❡ Bound Feet

Dear China:

Listen, your foot man is here at last under the silk trees in the land of bare bulbs and no cleavage. This is an enormous reservation with a fifty watter over the main street, but, as Marco Polo said, "I have not told the half of what I saw."

Last night at the train depot two exotic oldies with bound feet hobbled down the stairs in front of me, their elbows out wide for balance. I should have mimicked their miniature moves, by nature, but instead I carried their tattered bundles to the curb. No one, not even you in the best of times, would want lotuses that small, four inches toe to heel.

The new sounds of this place hold me for ransom at some alien border. On one side there are the teachers, the decadent missionaries of this generation, and on the other side, invented traditions, broken rituals, wandering lights, ear readers, and headless ghosts on the dark roads. Here, now, alone on the line, huge beetles maul the rusted screen with their thick brown wings and small mosquitoes wail behind my neck and then bite me on the ears and knuckles, nowhere else.

In the bedroom and near the wide window there are hidden sounds, hollow whispers from the cool concrete.

13

Even the silence bothers me, no whacks from the summer wood, no motors at night, no sirens. Dreams and the urban wither haunt me the most this first hot and humid night.

Thousands of small bats come home to their narrow cracks in the walls around the windows. Their night rolls over to the sparrows, the few that survived the revolution.

Remember that night on the reservation when we were alone in the woods, on that natural mount, and we heard whispers? Listen, last night was like that time on the mount but the voices came to me in dreams, and then later at the window.

We were on the desert silk roads, surrounded by mountains. You buried your toes in the hot blue sand and then the scene turned cool and we were at a glacial stream with luminous animals and birds.

Actually, this dream started much earlier on the plane while I was reading a book about the first explorers on the old silk roads who looted the temples and ruins in the ancient cities on the rim of the Taklamakan, and somehow, over the ocean, the words became a real desert scene. I was there, amused at first, but when I tried to hold the words down, a voice echoed from the page. The plane was transformed into a mansion, then a mountain, and the passengers became bears. The wind howled over the white poplars and the camels shuddered until the woman in the seat next to me asked several personal questions.

"Have you ever seen bound feet?"

"Yes," I said and nodded my head with a smile, certain that she would ask me, with some hesitation, the when and where.

"When?"

"Here, on this very flight."

"Where?"

"There, that woman with the narrow high heels, see how her toes are turned under?" The woman turned her face and then she tucked her feet under the seat. "Notice, however, that few men are aroused by those twisted toes."

China, she wanted to know about you and why you were not with me, and what it would be like to be a teacher here. How the hell was I supposed to know, we were still in the air. She hauled me back from dream scenes with her narrow realities, back at the moment a secret was about to be revealed to me. She held me down to the words, a good tourist.

I finished the book before we landed at Beijing and thought nothing more about it until late last night when I arrived at my new apartment. Time crowds me now, but these words need me here to hold down this place.

Egas Zhang, the director of the foreign affairs bureau, met me at the airport and escorted me back to Zhou Enlai University at Tianjin, which is about two hours by train from Beijing.

Egas chain-smokes and smiles over each word. His cheeks curl, rise and fall, even when he listens, and he punctuates his thin head to the right, the side he favors in conversations, the side he pockets one hand. He never gave his hand, his right hand never appeared last night. House proud translator with a colonial name, but at the same time he seems worried to be seen with a foreigner.

Egas Monitz, he told me, from the side of his mouth as we walked to the train, was a Portuguese doctor who was the father of the lobotomy and who won a Nobel Prize. Later, and in the same tone of voice, he asked me for deer antler, bear paws, and gallbladders from the reservation. Such aphrodisiacs are as rare as hen's teeth here.

Egas carried my two boxes of books to the apartment and then he surprised me with a cash advance. He counted the crisp bills three times, bobbed his head in time, a hesitant kowtow dance, and scurried down the stairs like some rodent. Later, I mocked his sinister sidewinder smile in the

15

high bathroom mirror. Even the sink is too high, the paranoid builders of this guest house must have imagined we were huge barbarians.

So, from bare bulbs, bound feet, colonial names, these high mirrors, this is a stranger place than we ever imagined that night last month back on the reservation.

The desert dreams called me back from this small apartment. I tried to roar in a panic hole, to hold me down like a printed word, but the wind dried my tongue and teeth. Then a luminous man dressed in a white silk coat chased me through the Jade Gate at Dunhuang and over the old cities buried on the silk roads. Below, the deserts turned and boiled, the Gobi, Lop Nor, and Taklamakan, between the Tien Shan mountains in the north and the Kun Lun in the south. There were whole cultures and cities under the fine sand. Deeper, there were columns of poplars, gardens and high mansions; peach, plum, and apricot orchards, all in bloom. The ancient cities of Korla and Aksu opened on the north road, Dandanuilik, and Khadalik, and the Kingdom of Khotan on the south silk road.

China, there were these incredible episodes in the dream that seemed to have something to do with my being here, now, in the present. The first dream drew me close to a bright light which seemed like a star at first. I could feel the heat on my face, but it was a fire on the balcony of the apartment, a fire bear, a shaman. The bear rumbled in the fire and drew me closer to the rail, and then, when my face seemed to burn, a pleasant sensation overwhelmed me. No fear, I reached for the bear, to be the bear, the fire, but when my arms touched her maw, the light withered. There, in the dark, a small terra cotta figure of a humanoid bear stood near the window. I touched the warm figure and mosquitoes swarmed on my knuckles.

The bear appeared once more but this time she led me to the Kingdom of Khotan where she showed me several bear shamans on a mural from the silk cultures. One fire bear wore a black opal ring surrounded with faceted azure-blue stones. She told me that bears mined blue jade and the rare lapis lazuli at secret places and traded the stones on the silk roads. The bear wore a small blue rabbit on a chain around her neck.

The stones burned on the concrete, on the curtains, on a torn map taped to the wall near the balcony door, on the collar of my shirt over a chair, and then flashed on the mirror over the bureau. The luminous stones multiplied, moved in the distance like lanterns on a mountain trail, and then vanished.

The mosquitoes returned to the screen for a minute, no more, and then I was alone on the south silk road. I could feel her heat, smelled wet hair behind me, and then the bear touched me on the shoulders with her paws. Two claws were broken. I tried to stay awake this time, to separate myself from the events in the dream. I focused on the sound of a steam engine in the distance and the mosquitoes on the screen. The sounds seemed real, in the present, but the bed and the room would not return.

The bear led me into another mansion buried on the desert. She was silent when we passed mountain scenes, stone people and wild fires on murals, bears with monkeys on their shoulders, monkeys with bats and lotus flowers embroidered on the backs of their coats, and at the end of the wide murals there was an old man with butterflies on his hands.

China, no shit, he winked at me.

The shaman told me that the mountain bear women saved the first silk cultures from evil. The old stone man, she told me, lived with a bear woman and their descendants became healers in tribal cultures around the world.

At the end of the murals, behind a wide door, there were baskets filled with bear bones and blue stones, and thou-

17

sands of manuscripts, histories of the shaman bear cultures from the mountains that surrounded the deserts. She pushed me into the room, closer to the bones, and told me to choose one birchbark manuscript to take with me. Outside, she opened the scroll and held me to the secrets.

China, this is hard to believe, but the figures and marks on the birchbark were the same as those on the tribal medicine scrolls from the reservation. There were shaman bears and humans with lines from their hearts and mouths. The whole scene was unbelievable, tribal visions on birchbark this far from our woodland. The fire bear told me some of the stories on the scroll, the histories of this nation, from the monkey origins to the revolutions, even the persecution of scholars, and the new capitalism, it was all there. But the future stories, what would become of this nation, she told me to read later.

China, a stupid thing happened to me between the desert mansion and this apartment. I hitched a ride with a shrouded woman on a horse-drawn wagon. The slow movement and the sound of the horse lulled me to sleep on a load of fresh vegetables. Believe this or not, I dreamed I was asleep in a dream, and when I woke up in the apartment, I had forgotten the manuscript on the back of the wagon.

The mosquitoes followed me back in memories to the desert, and now, I can even smell the earth, beets, and cabbages, on that wagon, but the birchbark manuscript is lost.

So, strange things are happening to me here, even on the first night. I have no idea what this place looks like in bright light. The last bats return to the concrete. I heard the sound of a cat, then ducks and chickens in the distance. Mosquitoes at the screen are more desperate at the end of the night.

Your feet come to mind,

Griever de Tianjin

ℊ Holosexual Clown

Warrior clowns imagine the world and pinch their time from those narrow scratch lines dashed between national politics and traditional opera scenes.

This clown, old but seldom stooped, bailed from a faded landscape, unlocks the campus gate at dawn, starts a charcoal fire in a small brazier, and then he totters over the line with two bright butterflies embroidered on the lapels of his blue opera coat.

"Wu Chou, Wu Chou," the children chant from their baskets and spacious sidecars, and some lean out to touch his lapels and the golden butterflies in a natal light. Even a tired peasant, the first to move through the gate that morning, saluted the winsome warrior from his horse cart loaded with platform poles.

China Browne followed the cart from the bus terminal to the campus. She waited outside the gate, a writer at the scratch line, with an invitation to interview a warrior clown about Griever de Hocus, the trickster teacher who liberated hundreds of chickens at a local street market and then vanished last summer on an ultralight airplane built by her brother. Once there, she would continue her research on Alicia Little, past president of the Natural Foot Society.

China folded her arms beneath her breasts and lowered her head to duck a cloud of dust; the street sweepers, two women with white cotton masks, wheeled their brooms down the road as close as they could come to a foreigner.

Wu Chou waited for the dust to pass and then he waved the writer over the line and into the small brick house near the gatepost. China brushed her hair, patted her blouse, and with a tissue, she daubed her teeth, nose, and cheeks.

"China lovers strain at the windows like flies," he said and circled the low backless chairs until she seemed comfortable with his voice and dramatic gestures. "The missionaries and tourists praise the obvious, plastic shoes, steam locomotives, and our ever-black hair, in their clever trinities."

Wu Chou studied China Browne as he circled the chairs: the slant of her shoulders, the round wrinkles on her elbows, the curve of her neck, ears, nose, and her small hands spread like leaves over a miniature tape recorder. She wore white cotton trousers and a pleated blouse with blue sailboats printed in broken rows over her low breasts. Her head seemed to rise with a common pleasance, but her fingernails were trimmed too close, and when she smiled a thin scar creased the right side of her wide brown forehead. He smiled and pinched the humid air near her face, around her dark hair.

China has three unrivaled worries and two obsessions. She is enchanted with the wild energies of smaller men and she is fascinated with pictures of bound feet. As a child she bound her feet and earned her given name; she folded bright blue bandannas around her toes and moved at night on ceremonial lotus feet to exotic places in the world. Once or twice a week, when she is lonesome, she draws silk ribbons between her toes, an unusual method of meditation.

"Most flies bounce on both sides of the pane, but tricksters are different, Griever de Hocus was different." Wu

Chou tapped the brazier and watched the scar appear and disappear on her forehead.

China worries about bad blood, small insects near her ears, and those wild moments when she loses connections with time. She is worried that she could be suspended without a season, severed from the moment; these fears have delivered her to the whims of clowns and the vicarious adventures of tricksters. She aimed the microphone at his face and leaned to the side to listen, like an animal at the window.

"Griever was holosexual," said the warrior clown.

"No, not gay."

"Holosexual, not homosexual," he emphasized. "Griever, you see, was the cock of the walk, and he seemed to love the whole wide world, he must have. . . ."

"Well, not the whole world."

"Listen, he was unbelievable, but he freed birds and he never picked flowers, you can write about that." Wu Chou paused to pinch the air around his head. "But the world gave him so much trouble for his time." He pitched his head forward, smiled, and placed a small kettle of water on the brazier. "Griever was a mind monkey."

"Mind monkey?"

"Yes, a holosexual mind monkey," he said and cocked his head to explain. "Griever loved women, heart gossip, stones, trees, and he collected lost shoes and broken wheels."

Wu Chou hunched his shoulders and turned his head to the side, a simian elocution pose from a scene in the comic opera. He raised his hands, wrinkled his nose, and pinched the smoke in the air around her shoulders.

"Holosexual indeed," she said and brushed her sleeves.

"Griever was the first foreign teacher to arrive that summer," he continued, "he endured the air pollution, the water, and the crowds, but not the foreign affairs bureau."

The warrior clown crouched near the brazier to fan the fire. He leaned closer, poured two bowls of black tea, and then he smiled wide and turned his head from side to side until she noticed two miniature butterflies on the loose wrinkled skin below his ears, like those embroidered on the lapels of his opera coat. She watched the insects dance and responded with a polite smile and gentle applause.

The brick house was shrouded under deep sculptured eaves. The room was bare with three backless chairs around the brazier, a polished leather holster, and a metal box on a narrow counter over a window. The wide wooden door had been removed and then burned during the first winter of the revolution. Crickets held the four points of the room and spiders molded the stained corners at the ceiling. Green katydids paused at the threshold in their season but never entered the room.

China watched his hands move in the smoke.

The warrior clown, a master of theatrical gestures, pinched the sun from his summer memories, from his maw and dark crotch, from faded tattoos, and a collection of uncommon names.

"Tianjin is a broken window," he announced with one finger on his ear. "Dreams retreat to the corners like insects, and there we remember our past in lost letters and colonial maps, the remains of foreign concessions.

"Look around at the architecture, the banks and hotels, the old names have disappeared but we bear the same missions in our memories." He laughed and disturbed the butterflies under his ears.

"Your accent is perfect," she said and then pinched her chin too late to hold back the last word. Her hand trembled.

"Colonial excellence," he mocked.

"Forgive me, please." She turned slantwise from one

cheek to the other on the narrow wooden chair and brushed the dust from her white shoes.

"We surrendered to the first missionaries," he said and then paused to hail a government official who was chauffeured through the gate in a black limousine. "We were students at the Nankai Middle School with Hua Lian and Zhou Enlai, but now we speak a rather formal and footsore language."

"Premier Zhou Enlai?"

"Indeed, and we practiced new words on the run," he said. "We followed visitors to the parks and picked on their best euphemisms and colonial metaphors, and we even dared to pursue unusual phrases into forbidden restaurants."

Wu Chou supped from the bowl. Steam rose from the hot tea and fogged the small round spectacles high on his nose. "But now, since the revolution, we talk back on hard chairs and wait to translate new verbs from the trick menus."

Wu Chou, which means warrior clown, a name he earned from the classical theater, was an actor before the revolution. He is remembered for his performances as the Monkey King in the opera *Havoc of Heaven*. When he was too old to tumble as an acrobat, he studied the stories of tricksters and shamans in several countries around the world. He returned home to teach, but the communists banished him to a *laogai*, a political prison farm, in the north where he planted trees and attended chickens. The trees were words in poems, he remembers, and the birds became characters he courted in interior operas. A decade later, past retirement and keen on common fowl, his reputation as a scholar and warrior clown was restored, and he accepted a simple sinecure as the overseer of the electronic portal at the main entrance to Zhou Enlai University. He starts the world there now and measures the thin cracks in his memories at dawn.

"Griever came back from the street market that first morning whistling 'The Stars and Stripes Forever' with blood and feathers on his shoes," he said as he pushed the button to open the gate for a wagon loaded with bricks.

"What on earth happened?"

"Griever freed the chickens and a cock spilled the blood," he said and held his mouth open. "He became the master of chicken souls, and that cock, stained with blood, followed him back to the campus."

"Not blood, no more blood, please."

"Griever was a mind monkey, remember that, he was a real holosexual clown in his own parade," said the warrior with a wide smile. His teeth were uneven, stained from black tea.

"But tell me, was he ever evil?"

"Never evil, never, never," he chanted at the rim of the tea bowl. "Cocks never follow devils, cocks chase devils, that cock chased some teachers from the guest house."

China was insecure, she crossed her arms and twisted one foot behind the other. She rocked from side to side on the chair and looked out the wide door toward the gate. The new trees were restrained at the wall, unnatural in the dust and charcoal smoke.

Silence.

Wu Chou reached for the small metal box near the leather holster on the narrow counter over the window. He dusted the box, opened it with care, and then he sorted through the contents, several dozen photographs.

"Look, look at this one here," he said as he moved behind the writer. He leaned over her right shoulder and presented a photograph.

"The same suede saddle shoes, he loved those shoes and those pleated trousers, he wore them on the reservation,"

24

she said and pointed at the color print. "He wore those when we first met at King's College Chapel in Cambridge." She held the print closer and studied the trickster. "He found a luminous statue somewhere in the choir stalls there, who could resist that man?"

"Griever was a natural clown," he said. "See, we painted his face white, with red and gold, for a rainbow celebration with the other foreign teachers."

Griever stood on one foot near the gatepost with a bamboo pole raised over his head. He wore a bright lemon raglan coat and loose blue trousers. His face was blurred in each print, but the trees, strangers at the gate, even the old warrior clown, appeared in sharp focus.

"What is this, here, in this print?"

"Horsehair duster."

"No, no, not the duster."

"What then?"

"This, here, he never wore a sporran on the reservation," she said and pointed with her little finger. She wore a beaded bracelet, the same color as the veins on her hands.

"Griever wore a holster," the clown responded as he leaned closer to her shoulder, so close that she could smell garlic and feel his warm breath. His cheek touched her dark hair from behind. He told her stories about the holster and watched the rise of her breasts, warm and brown, over the blue sailboats. When his small rough hand brushed the bare back of her neck she shivered and returned the photographs.

China stopped the recorder and moved to the door where she stood in the frame with her hands behind her neck. Her shadow coasted over the concrete, over the chairs, and folded like a child on the back wall. The clown leaned in the charcoal smoke and pinched a trace of her brown breasts from the floor. When she turned in the frame her shadow broke from his reach.

25

"Why would he need a holster?"

"To shoot clocks."

"Not the market cock?"

"Clocks, clocks, he loved cocks, he was a cock master, but he hated clocks," he said in a loud clear voice. "He carried a holster to shoot time, time on the clock."

"What was in the holster?"

"Pictures from wild histories," said the clown. He removed the scroll from the holster and turned the rough white paper past scenes with teachers, students, bats, and luminous bodies, and chickens at the street market. The warrior clown turned past scenes with a black opal, a small blue rabbit, a woman with a scar on her cheek, and a blind woman with painted cheeks; past swine on a basketball court, willow trees, small brick houses, blue bones, and ultralight airplanes.

"Wait, the woman with the scar, who is that?"

"Hester Hua Dan," he said and lowered his head. "She is the woman no one wanted him to find." Wu Chou rewound the scroll and closed the holster.

The old clown pinched the air and whispered to her shadow as she sliced past the window. Two spiders waited near the narrow crack in the pane; fine dust stretched their webs 'on both sides of the window.

♌ Jade Rabbit

Griever watched the bats flutter in wide circles and then vanish at narrow seams beneath the eaves. He was perched at the window, alone in the concrete guest house at the crack of dawn.

China opened in pale blue smoke.

The shadows heaved on the lanes and wambled between the rows of low brick houses. A white cat pounced on broad leaves in the courtyard below the balcony of his apartment.

Griever waited for the last bats to return and then he eased his rigid legs down from the window sill. He was short, not much taller than the students he would teach, and facile, but he was tired and his moves that morning were stilted; he paused over the scars on the red painted floor where the previous teachers had pushed the furniture from one side of the room to the other.

He remembers uncommon landscapes, the cleaves and rutted patterns from his childhood. His memories are bundled and marked with emblems, and he imagines stories about other people from their scars, prints, carved hearts, crude crosses gashed on trees; new cultures scored on desks and public corridors, and from natural wrinkles, faults on faces and the earth.

"People who pick flowers catch bad memories," he

warned a woman on the plane over the ocean. "Listen, imagination is the real world, all the rest is bad television."

"We never, never, watch television," she said and twice tied threads on a needlepoint, a column of bright lilies.

Mosquitoes whined in the small apartment. The pale green walls were moist, blistered, and darksome mold laced the high corners in the uneven concrete rooms. Brown ants gathered at the sugar stains on the bare book shelves. He heard his wild heart beat at the window.

Griever crossed the scars on the floor and his heartbeat doubled in the hollow bathroom; breathless in the cold shower. He dressed and hurried down the carpeted stairs to the entrance hall. There, he fastened the polished leather holster to his waist and wheeled through the double doors into the middle land.

Outside, in the pale blue light, he circled a brackish fish pond and watched a woman swim from one side to the other. She wore a black rubber helmet and mask and moved like a monster beneath the stone bridge. He waved twice, four times, when she raised her arms to stroke the thick dark water.

Griever saluted the old clown with the butterflies on his lapels and then he danced over the line at the campus gate. His heart pounded near the dark canal and came to rest on the crowded street. He stumbled at the curb, fumbled simple gestures on the unfamiliar road, and paused for pardons in a firm set of exotic faces; he even turned to accept apologies from those who clipped him on the run.

The cicadas droned with the first heat of the sun, natural harmonies over the roar of the trucks and diesel buses. His fingers were swollen at the bottom of his deep pockets.

Chinese women peddled apples and pears on the street. Two thin men sold *shibajie*, fried twists of dough, from narrow stalls at the corner; their white coats were smirched at the collar and pockets.

28

Griever watched several transactions from the sidelines and then he moved to make his first purchase. He paid for two and plucked the twists of bread from the thumbs of the man behind the counter. The sweet taste of lard reminded him of winter on the reservation.

Griever was thirteen when his family was relocated by the federal government. That first week on the coast his new urban friends sold him a subscription to peep at the narrow rear windows of the motel near the reservoir. He had listened to the sounds of sex on iron beds and in the dark corners of cabins on the reservation, but he had never seen the act in the flesh until he paid for a regular perch at the back of the motel. One night when he could smell the ocean at the window, he watched a white man, dressed in a maroon leisure suit, have sex with a small luminous woman; her breasts were scarred. The man mounted her from behind at the end of the bed.

Griever waited for several months at the rear window for the luminous woman but she never returned. When he was older he rented that same motel room and imagined that he touched the scars on her breasts and watched from the window at the same time.

Griever ate one twist of dough and waited for the traffic to break when a woman with broad shoulders brushed him from behind. She enunciated her apologies with practiced tones and then she moved like a dancer between trucks and buses, horses and handcarts, to the other side of the street.

"Wait, wait," he shouted over the diesel roar when he saw the scar on her cheek. He waved his hands and lurched like an arboreal animal through the machines.

The woman hurried to the bus stop on the corner, unaware that she was pursued by a foreigner. He touched her shoulder from behind and when she turned he smiled, opened his hands, and dropped the second twist of dough.

"You must be a teacher," she said with a polite smile but

held her distance. He nodded, breathless, relieved that she understood his position. He watched her hands move and then her cheeks; a small muscle twitched at the corner of her mouth where the scar started.

She moved back to avoid his attention and then leaned from the curb to look for the bus. He moved closer but she looked past him down the road, avoided his silent watch. Her cheeks were translucent, the color of mellow persimmons under rain; the moist scar was darker.

"Two blocks down, free market there," she said and pointed with both hands, "vegetables, chickens, much to eat." She wore a small jade rabbit on a chain around her neck.

Griever was pushed from behind; he touched her shoulder and cheek when he reached to hold his balance. The man who pushed him cleared his throat and spat near the trickster. He was dressed in new plastic clothes, a white shirt and blue trousers, pellucid sandals over thin brown socks with red toes. The man carried a black case with the seal of a panda bear on the side; the zipper was broken.

"Well, pardon me," the trickster mocked. He turned and lost his place in line; the woman with the jade rabbit and the scar moved ahead. When the rear doors of the bus opened he was pressed to the side.

"Cuse me, cuse me, peess, moneen," said the man with a short hiss between each word. When he smiled his mouth opened too wide; oversized teeth, white foam, bluish flesh, and bits of green food were exposed.

Griever altered his thin smile from one cheek to the other. He tried to rush back in line but the serried race was sealed, impenetrable. He moved around the bus and asked for her name at each window. People laughed but no one answered; at the end the man turned back, smiled once more, hissed, and then he closed his mouth at the same time the double doors snapped shut. The bus lurched from the curb.

30

¶ Peking Nightingale

Griever resolves his bother and concern in the world with three curious gestures: he leans back on his heels and taps the toes of his shoes together; he pinches and folds one ear; and he turns a finger in search of a wild strand of hair on his right temple. The third habit, he wrote to a former teacher, was his search for one "metahair, the hair that transforms impotencies, starved moments, even dead-ends."

China pressed and the man with the panda case demanded three gestures that first morning on the street. The trickster tapped his toes, pinched his ear, and pulled a single strand of hair from his temple. The nation was transformed near the bus stop when he twisted the hair between his fingers. He crossed the old men spread like broadsides over red benches in a park; the men turned over, shirts open to the waist, trousers high, and nodded their thin wet necks. Children peed through wide slits in their pants on the hard flower beds. Three women faced the fruit trees and exercised their stout arms and thighs, secular ecstasies at dawn, cordons on the garden mass.

China rushed over him from the shadows and smoke. Colors burst from the wild hair between his fingers and late flowers peeled open in the poison air. He moved back over culture lines, a shaman over the veils and hollow beams, down the stairs in ritual time, down to the meadows where animals and trees heal in the same language. His friends listened to the trickster stories, moments pinched from hard realities, but did not understand those sudden reversals in time and memories. He would reveal how much he missed that woman on the bus, how the sun died in diesel exhaust, and how she remembered his nose pressed on the windows.

Griever lectures, with his hands in constant motion, that we are "luminous when we dream." Imagination, he believes, "is what burns in humans. We are not methods to be discovered, we are not freeze-dried methodologies. We remember dreams, never data, at the wild end." The trickster remembers the luminous thighs that coast down the rough bark on the fruit trees into the vast wet shadow pools behind the benches in the park.

Two small horses clapped in slow motion through a wide intersection at the end of the garden. The trickster dropped the strand of hair and followed the horses on a narrow street under canopies of wet clothes stretched on bamboo poles to an outdoor market. He followed a peasant on a wagon loaded with fresh vegetables.

Griever took the winter melons in hand, commended the sweet potatoes and cabbages, palmed the small hard pears, saluted a plump child in a sidecar, and mocked a bird in a bamboo keep. The pears were cold, the child was staid, but the bird responded to the trickster.

The Peking Nightingale followed him from bar to bar as he circled the cage. The babbler pitched her head to the side and thrust her blunt orange beak at the barbarian. The cage, suspended from a small fruit tree, was built like a temple, a miniature joss house with mirrors and bird furniture. Overhead, white towels were spread on the branches to dry.

Griever whistled a low air. The keep moved and the

temple mirror reflected a small blot of his face. The babbler marched from the side bars to the rood beam, and then to the crown of the keep. There, she waited upside down in silence, her green crest feathers flexed. Griever was warmed; he moved even closer and imagined that he was small in his smile. He soughed and pretended to touch his miniature nose to the bars; he snorted, once, twice, through the bars. The bird threw her beak back and hissed at the monster. The rapid beat of her heart moved the soft golden plumes on her breast.

"Listen, little babbler, here's the plan," he mumbled to the bird. He moved his lips close to the temple door. "When the latch trips open, beat it back as fast as you can to that park on the corner, we can talk there."

The Peking Nightingale hissed louder at the huge face at the temple bars. "This is it," he said and expanded his nostrils. The trickster took a deep breath and raised the brass latch with his nose. The babbler held to the crown, unmoved when the miniature gate opened. Meanwhile, a plume tickled his nose; he sneezed, and moved the cage. Scared, the bird lost her place and dropped through the gate to freedom. She swooped down near a child in a bamboo carriage, soared, turned wide around the street market, over the vegetables, and bounced from towel to towel in the tree over the cage.

Griever cheered the liberation flight. He leaned back on the heels of his shoes and tapped his toes together, unaware that dozens of people had paused near the tree to watch the foreigner whisper to a caged bird. The babbler flew back to her secure keep in the dead tree; people moaned, some applauded, others turned and shook their heads with disappointment. Several people clucked their tongues at the bird.

"When a bird gets too big, it breaks the cage," warned the trickster. He locked the keep and turned it around several times.

¶ Matteo Ricci

Griever leaned back on a plane tree in a patch of shade and watched three chickens bleed to death on the other side of the market. He tried to warn the cockerel and two white hens but it was too late. In minutes the dead birds were boiled, plucked, paid, and carried naked from the market.

Griever opened his holster, drew the scroll, and with three colored pens he resurrected the dead chickens. The cockerel strutted across the rough paper with hairless humans bound to his shanks. He turned the scroll, past the human with a blue star tattooed on his hand, and painted a proud white cock leading all the caged hens to freedom.

Griever is a mixedblood tribal trickster, a close relative to the old mind monkeys; he holds cold reason on a lunge line while he imagines the world. With colored pens he thinks backward, stops time like a shaman, and reverses intersections, interior landscapes. The lines and curves in his pictures are dance, meditation moves, those silent gestures in an opera scene. Prevalent time and place are dissolved in ecstasies, but there is much more to this trickster than mere transcendence. Griever discovers events, an active opera and an audience, all at once on rough paper. He paints the comic resolutions back into tragic dances; he paints to find a patron, and he found one in the white cock with the feathered shanks.

34

The chicken cutthroat at the counter wore a black rubber apron and an ominous sneer; his cheeks stretched, and his nose flattened. The skin on his hands and face was hard and scabrous, cracked on his lips and thumbs. He reached for a lean hen in one of the wire cages stacked on the street.

With one hand the cutthroat turned the chicken upside down; he laced his fingers around the neck, leg, and one wing of the hen, and with his other hand he whished a stained blade beneath the neck feathers. Dark blood splashed in a metal basin on the wooden counter. Blue flies circled the blood soaked feathers. The bird blinked once, twice, three times, wild near the end; one eye warned the witnesses in the audience. The bird scratched the token earth in space with one free leg; each feather extended in an escape flight from slow death. When the claws curled and the eyes clouded over, the bird was scalded in a barrel and plucked clean on the street. Plumes gathered in the trees, dried on the brick walls, on handcarts pulled through the market. The chicken was tied to the back rack of a bicycle; some naked birds were carried on nooses, their claws seemed outsized.

Cutthroat drank warm chicken blood.

Griever clipped a wedge of cuticle from his right thumb too close. He shivered and a thin line of blood spread beneath the short nail. He pressed his thumb to his lips and tongue and counted the chickens he would liberate that first morning at the market. He counted aloud, seventeen hens stowed in four crude wire cages and one proud cock tied to a short tether.

Griever pinched his ear once more, considered the landscape, holstered his scroll, and sliced through the free market crowd to the chickens. Conversations trailed him to the counter.

"Wai guo ren, wai guo ren, the foreign devil, the foreign devil," the cutthroat murmured with suspicion. Few foreigners visited the street market; teachers and other visitors were served their meals at hotels or in special guest houses.

Blood had spilled from the shallow basins and coagulated at the outer rim of the counter near the cages. The hens were nervous. Griever touched his ear, and then pinched his nostrils closed. The brackish smell of boiled feathers tickled his nose and settled deep in his throat. He coughed, pitched his head to the side and spat near the cages; his phlegm curved wide and hit a chicken on the neck. The other hens pecked at the thick spittle as it slid down the soiled white feathers.

The chicken cutthroat turned and waved his short arms like a sorcerer in unnatural flight. Black and white plumes stuck to his rubber apron. Griever overlooked the chickens, spread his arms wide and waved back at the cutthroat. He flapped hard several times, and then, pretending to be surprised, he looked down at his feet, shrugged his shoulders and smiled. At first the cutthroat seemed amused, but when he landed at the counter he snickered over the basins of blood and flashed two bright silver teeth, both incisors. When he spoke, fine lines trailed from his wide mouth like cracks on an old porcelain vessel. He pointed to the foreigner, turned his head to the right, a sudden movement that shifted his black hair, and muttered to his assistant, his epigone, who chortled back, as she poked at the hot coals under the barrel.

Cochin China, the prime cock at the market, posed over the hens. The feathers on his shanks shrouded the crude noose that fastened him to the wire cages. He strutted and danced in place, extended his short wings, shook his wild orange wattle, and carried on as usual, the natural domination of the hens, despite the short tether.

The cutthroat reached for the cock. On the back of his hand there was a large blue star. Griever admired the raw tattoo; he drew uneven angles in space with his middle finger, erased the invisible star, and then started over when the cutthroat untied the tether on the cock.

"Free the birds," said Griever.

"*Ji wang, ji wang,*" the cutthroat repeated several times with a pinched smile. The crowd around the counter laughed when he spoke, and laughed more when his assistant chortled over the fire. Cutthroat tipped his head to the crowd.

"How much for the whole flock?"

"*Ji wang, ji wang. . . .*" The cutthroat wrapped the tether around his wrist and pushed the cock down the counter toward the foreign devil.

Cochin China shuddered, flicked his sickle feathers in place, restored his balance once more, a constant struggle with humans, and then the proud cock burst into short flight to the end of the tether and crashed on the blood soaked counter. The hens thrust their heads through twists in the wire cages and clucked in turns, a domestic summons to a primal dance.

Griever leaned back, tapped the toes of his shoes together, and asked the cutthroat how much it would cost to free all the chickens in the cages. He turned his pockets and presented cash, the total advance he had received the night before when he first arrived at the guest house. He spread the bills, tinted pictures of romantic workers and idealized industries, on the counter like a deck of cards.

"Take a card, any card, and count it twice," he said, not knowing the real value of the paper money. The crowd moved closer; several people counted with their fingers. "The best chickens chase the devil," said the trickster. He reached for the cock with one arm and drew him close to his chest; there, he soughed and whistled a tune from "The Stars and Stripes Forever." The cock marched in place and shit on his wrist.

37

"Cochin China, you are now ordained Matteo Ricci," the trickster announced with a flourish. "So, take that for a consecrated name and mind your manners."

The cutthroat leaned over the cash on the stained counter, his hands and face branded, mottled with chicken blood and feather barbules. He spelled out the cost of one bird, the cock, in slow finger signs. Spectators sighed, some nodded in agreement with the price. Cutthroat waited in silence, rested his fingers in space, like a minor actor in an opera, but the traditional colors on his face were contradictions. Red, the chicken blood, signified courage, and white hen feathers, the mask of death.

Griever did not understand the gestures. He pushed the cock aside, pointed at the chickens, and counted aloud the number on each of the bills. Matteo Ricci scratched at the crisp notes, one or two bills disappeared under his feathered shanks. The cutthroat picked up three bills, looked around the crowd for approval, and then he returned some change with a sneer. The cock seemed to understand; he moved farther from the cutthroat, stood in silence, his wattle shivered with each human gesture. Then the cutthroat turned with a twisted smile and pulled at the tether, but the cock crowed, flapped, and marched back down the counter to the end. The hens clucked low from their cages. More people gathered in close bands around the chicken counter.

Griever protested when the cutthroat reached for his blade. "No, alive, give me all of them alive," he cried as he took the tether and coaxed the cock down to the end of the counter near the cages; there, he tied the tether to his right thumb. "Matteo Ricci," he muttered to a man with a child on his shoulder, "will lead the liberation of these hens." The man understood nothing but he smiled; the child stared and then reached to touch the outsized nose on the foreigner.

38

Cutthroat stood in silence, the color drained from his face, his hands withered at his sides. Even the star tattoo drooped on his hand. He did not understand what the foreign devil wanted from the chickens, something more than food. He worried about evil forces and that his customers would be unsettled by the strange scenes, but the spectators were rather amused. More people gathered to watch the foreigner and the cutthroat, pressed even closer to the match over the counter. Matteo Ricci shook his radiant wattle with each utterance.

Griever demanded the release of the chickens. "Take the cash and turn those chickens loose, now, now, now," he said. His voice tripped higher with each word. Someone from the crowd spoke out and the cutthroat seemed to understand what the foreign teacher wanted, and as he understood, his sneer and flesh color returned to his hard round face. Poised over the chickens like a predator, the cutthroat pushed one black head down and through the wire and wrenched a nervous hen from the bottom of the cage.

Griever clapped and danced in circles at the counter. "More, more, liberate the whole flock," he boomed to the crowd and wagged his hands. He threw the last of his money on the blood soaked counter. The cutthroat was no less cautious; he counted with his fingers, slow and deliberate motions, the cost of the second bird, selected that amount, and then he handed the black hen over to the foreigner. The trickster held both shanks and pitched the nervous bird over his head into the street market crowd. When he raised his hands the tether tied to his thumb overturned the cock and stained the swell of his great white breast a second time.

Meanwhile, the free black hen floundered in flight and crashed on the head of a woman, no more than fifteen feet from the cages. The trickster laughed hard, so hard that he doubled over on the counter, stained his elbows, his nose close to the basins of blood. Matteo Ricci thrust his beak at his ears and dark hair.

Griever pinched his ear and spat near the cages. Frustrated, his humor turned sour; he demanded, in his loudest voice, the liberation of all the chickens. The trickster had painted these scenes; now, he moved with the cock in his own opera. His chest rippled, perspiration rolled from his armpits down his ribs, and his breath was short and sudden; even his vision blurred for an anxious moment. Then he moved back with the cock, back into the figures he had painted earlier on rough paper, back to a decided pose. The spectators never lost their smiles; no one seemed to notice the rash turn to meditation; at the same time, the children were restless and the cock crowed down the counter at the cutthroat.

Matteo Ricci chased the devils from the free market. The caged hens wheeled their heads from the familiar faces in the crowd back to their foreign liberator.

Chickens were expensive, compared to fish and pork, and most people at the counter could not afford the cost of fowl, except for special celebrations. Chicken liberation, then, was better understood as a comic opera. The audience was drawn to the trickster and his imaginative acts, not the high cost of chicken breasts. Mind monkeys, from practiced stories, would have done no less than emancipate the birds in a free market. Those who liberate, in traditional stories, are the heroes of the culture.

Cutthroat folded his arms beneath the rubber apron and stood in silence, not a monarch at the margins of a revolution, but a stubborn sorcerer, alone at the end of his scene in the opera. Small muscles twitched on his thick neck; masseter muscles shuddered, moved several black and white plumes on his cheeks and chin.

Matteo Ricci preened and hopped down the counter to

the end of the tether, turned and hopped back with a black feather in his radiant beak. The hens clucked with their heads stretched through the wires, and people in the crowd whispered about scenes in the other mind monkey stories. Privities rushed over the bloom, down two blocks on both sides of the market, over the cabbages, over the leeks and carrots, between the fish nooks, and onto the street dash at the end. People on bicycles heard the stories about the *wai guo ren*, the foreign devil, the outside or external person, and the evil cutthroat.

Griever smiled, a slow curve like a slice of melon on one side of his face. He mocked the whispers and the gestures of those around him and then he burst into wild laughter.

"Matteo Ricci rules from his tether," the trickster shouted with the nervous cock on his shoulder, "but he has no humor when his hens are prisoners."

The cutthroat remained silent, stoical behind his rubber apron which was covered with feathers. Black plumes twitched on his chin. His assistant was aroused by the whispers, the secrets she could learn, and she responded with laughter too. She chortled, danced, and thumped the sides of the cauldron until sparks shot out from the fire, water splashed over the sides.

An old woman notched through the crowd toward the counter. She carried the black hen high above her head. The old woman was too small to be seen at first, but people parted for the nervous beat of the bird. She bounced the chicken on the counter, wheedled the hen to be still, and then she leaned back into the crowd without a word. She wore a new blue coat, too thick for the late summer weather, buttoned high to her thin wrinkled neck.

"English, do you understand?" he asked. She cocked her head like a bird, and like his tribal grandmother. Both of them, he remembered, overdressed in summer. Peaches, who was born on a woodland reservation, pretended most of the time that she did not understand her trickster grandson. His urban mixedblood tongue, she snorted when he graduated from college, "wags like a mongrel, he's a wild outsider." Even at home on the reservation he was a foreigner.

The old woman stood at the border of the crowd, a silent wreath in a blue desert. She had the teeth of a child, small, even, and translucent. She leaned to one side, to an ancient wind, a natural pose, and then she laced her fingers behind her back and smiled.

Peaches posed like that too, and she wore false teeth once a week to the mission church. Griever mocked her when she worked in the garden without her teeth. She covered her sweet toothless smile with her small hands and stood to the wind in a plain print dress buttoned high on her neck.

Now, with his hands behind his back, he smiled back at the old woman who had returned the black hen. He mocked her moves too, her short minced steps back from the counter, back from the cock, back from the blood, back from the cutthroat and evil. No one laughed; her feet were bound when she was a child.

"Golden lotuses," the trickster said and pointed at her small feet wrapped in dark blue cloth. "Listen, my grandmother had wide feet but no teeth." His laughter was strained. People near the counter understood his gestures but not his words. Some frowned, others turned to leave.

Griever stooped to apologize to the old woman; he pleaded with open hands as he had pleaded with his grandmother when she misunderstood his indelicate humor. Peaches would forgive the uncoined trickster, she was in his blood, but she was seldom eager to recognize his imaginative survival stunts. He reached for the old woman and tripped the cock once more.

Matteo Ricci flapped in a wild circle to restore his balance at the end of the tether. When the cock turned he spilled a basin of blood and scared the black hen back to the cages. In the confusion, the old woman vanished in the blue desert.

Griever pinched his ear and climbed to the top of the wooden counter. He looked over the audience and called out several times for a translator. He waited, called again, but there was no response to his summons.

"*Kuku kuku*," the cutthroat intoned.

"No, no, listen, the cock *cockadoodledoos*."

"*Kuku kuku*."

"Would someone please tell this dildo in the rubber apron to free these chickens." He pointed to the cages and then waved his arms. The cock hopped in time with his gestures.

"We are not translators," responded a woman from the back of the audience, "but perhaps we could help, we could at least give it a good try." She moved forward, a tall blonde in a business suit. "We have a simple phrase book, would that help?"

"Who is we?"

"My friend over there."

"Who is she?"

"Sugar Dee, and my name is Jack."

"Jack, can you translate liberation?" he asked in a paternal tone of voice. He did not look at the blonde; he spoke to the audience.

"Liberation?"

"Yes, liberation, one word."

"The concept?"

"No, the word," he said, "we are the concepts."

"Oh dear, but we thought you were trying to buy a chicken," said the second woman who wore a thin print dress with huge orange poppies, one on each breast. Sugar Dee and the blonde stood at opposite ends of the counter. The two were industrial management consultants, invited to lecture at a special institute on the future of capitalism.

43

"This is a liberation, not a meal," he barked and strutted behind his cock down the blood soaked counter. "This is real, this is freedom, not some precious recipe."

"Liberate chickens, are you serious?"

"Serious?" He mocked her tone of voice, but still he spoke to the audience as he crouched on the counter with the cock tied to his thumb. "Look, Jack, here is the money, right here, so you tell me now, which is crazier for the same price, to free these chickens or bleed them to death over a basin?"

"Stop barking at me," said the blonde.

"Please, do you have the word?" Griever leaned toward the blonde, looked at her for the first time; his gestures were gentle, more personal. She moved closer to the chickens to avoid his attention.

"This must be a movie set," said Sugar Dee. She turned to the audience at the counter and smiled; she had been trained in the suburbs to surrender to the prince of movie pictures. This unusual moment rippled on her cheeks as she posed with slender hands on her wide thighs. Her nipples pipped two wild poppies on her dress.

"Tell the cutthroat here that I want to buy all of his birds, the hens in all four cages," said the trickster.

"Look, we are not translators," the blonde responded.

"Listen, Jack," he mocked with a smile, "look up 'free the chickens' in that little phrase book then, tell him that, tell him I will pay whatever he wants to free all the chickens."

"This is just a phrase book for tourists," the blonde pleaded. "There is no way I can translate that much, but even if I could I don't mind telling you that we would rather not get involved in this idiotic scheme."

"Do you like kittens?"

"Never mind."

"Pretend these are little kittens. . . ."

"The mongrel and the kittens," she whispered.

"The concept then," he said as he loosened the belt on his pleated trousers. He unbuttoned his red and gold checkered shirt and fanned his hairless chest with the tails. His saddle shoes were scuffed, rounded at the heels. The cuffs on his trousers dragged across the counter through the spilled blood.

"*Zi you*," said Jack.

"What?"

"*Zi you*, free."

"Why is everyone laughing?"

"Wait, it could mean seed oil too."

"Shit."

"Wait, how about this?"

"What?"

"*Kaide ji jian yu*," said Jack.

"*Ji jian yu*," the trickster repeated several times, and waves of laughter rushed over the counter. "What does that mean?"

"Open chicken prison."

"Fly, no eat," said the trickster, "look that up."

"*Cang ying bu chi*," she enunciated.

"*Cang ying bu chi*," he repeated and waved his arms down the counter, "fly, no eat chickens, *cang ying bu chi*."

Matteo Ricci bounced behind the trickster on the tether and pecked at the laces on his shoes. The audience laughed and mocked the mispronounced words.

"One more word," the trickster demanded.

"What now?"

"Cook, *bu* cook, *bu* cook, no cook," he chanted.

"The verb or the noun?"

"The word."

"*Chui shi yuan*."

"Once more, what was the word for chicken?"

"*Ji*," she whispered.

45

"*Cang ying bu chi ji*, fly no eat chickens," the trickster bellowed from the blood-soaked counter, "*bu chui shi yuan ji*, no cook chicken."

Matteo Ricci crowed behind the trickster and the audience twittered with amusement over his pronunciation; then, near the counter, wild laughter burst and spread down the street.

"Well, this is no movie set then, is it?" asked Sugar Dee. The poppies moved when she abandoned her theatrical pose. The crowd, she had decided, was not there for a movie scene.

Sugar Dee imagines movie sets when she does not understand a time or place. In a similar manner, she leans toward people she does not understand until she notices their imperfections and then she blinks her eyes and ends the scene. From a distance, she was attracted to the characters at the counter; and the cutthroat, in turn, was roused with lust. He moved closer to the white woman, watched the orange poppies.

"This is a chicken liberation, not a television talk show," the trickster shouted and tracked down the counter. "Free the chickens."

"Christ," exclaimed the blonde, "just our luck, ten thousand miles from home and we end up with the weirdies."

"Listen, do me a small favor," said the trickster as he backtracked on the counter, "look up the meaning of *ji wang, ji wang.*"

"*Wang, wang, wang*, is that a name?" The blonde mumbled and searched in the phrase book for the words. "*Ji, ji, ji wang.*"

Matteo Ricci shivered. The hens were nervous, their heads wobbled from side to side through the wire, like flowers in a thunder storm. Cutthroat sneered when he heard his words spoken with a barbarian accent.

"*Wang* means 'king,'" the blonde announced.

46

"King?"

"*Ji* means 'chicken,'" she said. "Now, what else?"

"Listen Jack, he called me king chicken," said the trickster. He scratched his bare stomach. "Now, what about those concepts."

"For the record, mister chicken king," said the blonde with her head cocked to the side, "what the hell are you doing with all these people?" Her blond hair spread across her dark shoulders, her lips were tight, unnatural as she spoke. Jack threw her hair back, wiped sweat from her neck, and waited for a response.

Griever pinched and folded his right ear and then his finger searched for a wild hair; he pulled it from his temple and rolled it between his fingers. The tall blonde and the other faces in the audience were transmuted from scenes on his scroll to a classroom in a public school. He was a child at his desk four rows from the back of the room.

¶ Griever Meditation

The science teacher demonstrated how electrical shocks stimulated the leg muscles of a dead frog. The common green frogs, captured over the weekend near the creek and held in a glass case, seemed to leap much higher dead than alive. The frogs were to be dissected once the teacher had desensitized the students with the scientific method. Some of the fifth grade girls were sick, their noses wrinkled like permanent cultural scars. The sick girls were allowed to leave the room, the first level of elimination in the scientific colonization of nature.

"Remember children," said the teacher as she hiked her thumbs high, a sign that she was about to release significant information, "some people eat frog legs and throw the rest away, and there are millions of frogs eaten by snakes and birds, and millions more are run over by cars, so these few here, the ones we are about to dissect this morning, you see, will not matter in the overall world of the frogs."

"Do frogs have science teachers?" Griever pressed his nose and one cheek hard against the glass case and watched the teacher move between the frogs inside.

The teacher ignored the question. She lowered her thumbs and moved to the chalkboard where she drew an outline of an enormous frog with legs extended. Then she slashed at the board with a stub of chalk, severed the legs, removed the heart and other organs, and heaped them on the side board. Later, she colored the enlarged organs with red, white, and blue chalk. The mineral dust stained her hand and the right pocket of her white coat.

"Do frogs know who they are?" Griever threw his question from a distance, over the case of live frogs. His teachers were critical of his manner, his deceptive tone of voice, and noted in official school records that he seldom took the time to listen to others. "Griever has an unusual imaginative mind," one teacher wrote, "and he could change the world if he is not first taken to be a total fool."

"Do you know who you are?" retorted the science teacher.

"Yes, a frog," he said from behind the case. The thick glass distorted the room, magnified faces, fingers, the organs on the chalkboard.

"But frogs, my little man," said the teacher as she wobbled in her white coat, "are not humans. . . . Here, we are humans."

Griever croaked like a free frog, someone croaked back, and then the other students laughed and hopped around the room.

"Then you must be the frog king," said the teacher. "Fear not, we will not dissect the king of the frogs this morning." She never smiled with students, her manner was too practiced in the classroom. She was rescued from total confusion when the bell sounded for morning recess. She told the other teachers in the lounge about the confrontation over frogs. One teacher, a tall blonde who dared to smoke narrow cigars, said, "The cause of his behavior, without a doubt, is racial. Indians never had it easier than now, the evil fires of settlement are out, but this troubled mixedblood child is given to the racial confusion of two identities, neither of which can be secured in one culture. These disruptions of the soul," she continued as she la-

49

bored over her cigar, "become manifest as character disorders. He is not aware of his whole race, not even his own name." She inhaled too much and choked. The other teachers were silent in the thick blue smoke.

Griever saw his father in his dreams near a slow curve in the river, on a small horse at the treeline, and pressed on the plastic outside the window; a creased photograph, an old souvenir. Wherever his father appeared, the son raised his voice in appreciation.

"Gypsy, what is a Gypsy?" Griever asked when he was told that his father came to the White Earth Reservation with a caravan named the Universal Hocus Crown.

"Handsome devil he was in bright flowered shirts," said his mother. Coffee, a descriptive nickname, told her son that she met his father at three places on the reservation: once behind the mission school, twice on the old government road, and three times in the ice barn near the lake, and then "the caravan was gone in less than a week." Coffee never understood his peculiar language, never even knew his real name, but she remembers his music, and she whistles his tunes. Coffee remembers, most of all, what he taught her about "griever time."

"Griever meditation," he told her in the dark, "cures common colds, headaches, heartaches, tired feet and tired blood." The Universal Hocus Crown sold plastic icons with grievous expressions, miniature grails, veronicas, and a thin instruction book entitled, "How To Be Sad And Downcast And Still Live In Better Health Than People Who Pretend To Be So Happy."

Coffee owes her old age and good health to "griever meditation" three nights a week. Griever, her eldest son, owes his name to this compulsive practice, but not much more.

"Griever de Hocus," the science teacher summoned in a

firm tone of voice. "Little man, where have you hidden our frogs?"

"No place," he promised.

"We must have the frogs to finish our experiment," she demanded with her thumbs held high, blood-red fingernails extended.

"The frogs are alive," he pleaded.

"Griever, give me the frogs this instant."

"The frogs all jumped over the fern," he explained as he turned toward the students, tapped the toes of his shoes together, and pinched his ear. Someone croaked and the students laughed and bounced at their desks.

"Mark my words, little man, you will be punished for this," said the teacher. She snapped her fingers and ground her teeth.

"Not by the frogs."

"This is a scientific experiment."

"Not by the frogs."

Griever packed the frogs on top of his lunch in a brown paper sack and liberated them one by one on the shaded cool side of the school building. There, in the gentle fiddlehead fern, he imagined that he became the king of the common green frogs.

Griever pinched and folded his ear once more; then he twisted a strand of hair on his right temple and pulled it out in front of the room. The school and the teachers were transformed in green; the landscape tilted to the right and slipped deep into the moist trees.

¶ Free the Garlic

"My cock is Matteo Ricci from Cochin China," the trickster announced with a flourish from the counter, "and I am
the king of the chickens."

"Who is Matteo Ricci?" asked Sugar Dee.

"Ricci was a missionary, an Italian Jesuit," the trickster
lectured, "and, believe it or not, he was taken prisoner
right here on the trail of the hare and hounds."

"When was that?"

"Three-hundred eighty-four years and seven days ago,
to be specific," he answered and winked at the cock on the
counter.

"Mister trickster, come down here for a minute." Sugar
Dee leaned forward and pressed her thighs to the counter;
her moist breasts heaved beneath the poppies.

"Call me Griever."

"Griever, what an interesting nickname," she said and
looked around at the audience. "Tell me, is there something real weird going on here?"

"Yes," he whispered.

"Tell me, you can tell me, what is it?" Sugar Dee leaned
closer to the counter to listen, closer to the trickster. The
cock brushed her hard nipples.

"See that man behind me?"

"Yes," she answered and looked over the cock.

"The man with the star tattoo."

"Where?"

"On his hand," he said close to her ear.

"Yes, the star is there."

"That man is an evil cutthroat."

"Evil cutthroat?"

"See this blood?"

"Not blood, no more chicken blood chatter," she moaned and moved back from the counter, but it was too late. Her waist was stained with blood, the poppies wilted.

Sugar Dee wrinkled her nose and stooped to touch the blood with a wad of tissue. The trickster hovered over the neck of her open dress.

When the cutthroat folded his rubber apron and rushed around the counter to assist the woman, the trickster folded his ear and seized the moment to liberate the chickens. He tucked the cock under his arm and leaped down behind the cages. The hens were excited; their heads wobbled through the twists in the wire. While the cutthroat driveled over the poppies, the trickster threw open the cages and freed the black and white hens. The birds beat their short wings in awkward flight over the audience.

"Free the pears."

"Free the garlic, make me rich," a peasant shouted. The trickster swaggered and whistled a march. Matteo Ricci wagged his orange wattle on the ride down the narrow market street.

Griever stopped near the vegetables to watch the chicken chase from a distance. The black hen, the first to be liberated, strutted from one end of the counter to the other, around the basins of blood. Several birds scurried through the crowd with their heads down, back to the cages. The woman in the orange poppies tried to catch two tattered white hens, the cutthroat close behind, but she abandoned pursuit when he touched one breast with his bloodstained

53

hand, the hand with the star tattoo. She screeched and beat a path with her head down low, like the hens, to the side of the tall blonde in the business suit.

Cutthroat cooled the fires, drained the basins of blood, counted the money spread on the counter, packed his rubber apron and his blades into the large wicker basket on the side of his bicycle, and then he pedaled from the street market, a free man in the middle of the morning.

Griever followed the orange poppies to the narrow canal at the other end of the street market. Sugar Dee walked and talked with the blonde, her voice strident. Patches of perspiration soaked through the thin dress at the small of her back, and down, a flower stuck to her cheeks. He watched the petals shiver, rise, and then fall with each step. She tossed her hair and avoided the trickster.

Griever pinched his ear and reached for the bloodstained poppies, but she leaped over a row of wicker baskets and blue clothes and vanished in the seams at the end of the street.

Matteo Ricci scratched at his arm and pecked at the buttons on his loose shirt when the trickster tumbled near a tree at the side of the canal. The tether slipped from his thumb and the cock wandered in the tall weeds near the water. The sun bloomed on the back of fish, broad leaves were overturned, and green shadows splashed on the hard blue earth.

Griever listened to the rapid beat of his heart over the roar of engines and the rattle of voices on the street. He was transformed from a flower to a bird, from a primrose to water ouzel in a warm rain. Plump children, wheeled over mountain meadows from the tribal past, were plucked from cosmetic chains, freed like small bears from a cold circus.

Griever turned a strand of hair between his fingers and dove deeper into the humoral water. He spread his fingers beneath the poppies, moved to the rise of her stomach.

54

Sugar Dee tossed her hair back, wide over his neck as he leaned on her shoulder close to her breasts. He became a woman there beneath her hair, and with thunder in her ears, she peeled the blossoms; she pulled her head down in the lambent heat, down on her breasts; dibbled and sheared her high nipples with the point of her tongue. She towed her flesh back from the cold and heard the cocks and animals on her breath.

❡ Mute Pigeon

Once a night, no matter where he rests, at hotels, guest houses, berths on a train, with friends or relatives, the trickster turns the mattress over and loosens the sheets before he sleeps. Griever learned this unusual practice from an old shaman who told grim stories about the dream thieves and the children who lose their dreams.

"Turn the mattress," she told the children on cold winter nights, "because lonesome white people with no shadows hound the tribes and capture our dreams." Tricksters and mixedbloods, she said, "lose their dreams when they talk too much in bed, their stories are sacked in the blood."

The white dream thieves had double trouble in the guest house because the maids there turned the mattresses over in the morning and never tucked the sheets.

Matteo Ricci was perched at the vanity mirror.

Griever turned the mattress and dreamed that he arrived at the train station late at night. The terminal was crowded and smelled of urine. The children who wavered in the dark were pushed through the gates, their little heads covered with white cloth cases. The inspector of midgets waited in the shadows to catch bourgeois deceivers; she pressed bodies to a measure on the wall. More than three feet paid

56

a whole fare. Women lowered their trousers, raised their dresses, at venereal disease inspection centers near the turnstiles. Cadres dressed in white coats and turbans touched each vulva; small blue animals with coarse hair and broad snouts were trained to sneeze over various diseases.

Griever was pushed to the turnstile and heard three animals sneeze. Men, in a separate line, faced the animals and lowered their trousers. The trickster resisted; he dropped back several times in his dream, and then the eager crowd forced him to the front. He watched the others, heard an animal sneeze, and held back at the turnstile. Those behind him shouted and raised their fists. The belt on his trousers would not open; the zipper broke. He could not find the fold in his underwear, he would urinate under too much pressure, but somehow he held his penis out and pushed it into the face of the blue animal on a crotch high pedestal. The animal snarled, her wet snout shivered over blunt blue teeth.

Outside, on the crowded street in front of the train station, dozens of men and women, dressed in bright uniforms, marched in circles and chanted slogans into copper megaphones.

"Remember our national policies, our proud new policies," the voices intoned, "we strive to better our lives, death to cats and dogs, one child, death to criminals, one child, death to venereal diseases, one child, death to capitalist roaders, one child, death to spiritual pollution, one child, no spitting, one child, no ice cream with barbarians, one child, no sex on the road, one child, no bright colors, one child, no decadent music, one child, no telephone directories, one child, the east is red."

A mute child followed the trickster through the crowd from the train station to the guest house. His dark face

57

appeared in mirrors, reflected in windows, bounced from light to water, and paused at critical intersections. No matter where the trickster turned the child was there.

The streets were narrow and black. Somehow he understood the language on the street, he heard his new voice, he could read signs, he understood train schedules, which buses to board, and where to cross the canal to the campus.

The trickster followed the mute child over loose pools of ancient dust, beneath two bare light bulbs, and twice around the pond. He paused at the entrance to the guest house, and then, with the mute child close to his side, he took the stairs two at a time to the third floor. When he unlocked the door to his apartment, the child leaped through the rooms in the dark, over the scars on the floor, and out to the small balcony. The mute child stood like an animal at the treeline; his eyes held the pale light from the crowded brick houses beyond the walls of the courtyard.

Griever pushed open the screen door and stood close to the child. The last bats dropped from their seams beneath the eaves. He smiled and the child smiled back; his teeth were short and uneven, his breath smelled of garlic. The child looked down and moved his bare feet from side to side on the concrete. He wore blue trousers tied at the waist with twine and a clean white shirt two sizes too large, buttoned to the neck. The child was warm, his face moist. Wild blue light seemed to burn at loose folds in his clothes.

Griever reached to touch the child but held his hand back, afraid that he would vanish. He gave the child a pencil and he drew several pictures on the smooth concrete. First he outlined a prairie schooner pulled by a small horse, and then a lake with an island and brick houses surrounded by several oversized swine. Near the screen door he made a man who wore a round mask with a wide evil smile. The man held bones in his hands.

Griever wrote to China Browne that the child was out there several hours, "silent and alone, with nothing but a pencil. When he blinked it seemed darker, his nostrils expanded from time to time, his feet and hands moved as he drew, but never more than a few inches.

"He examined my leather holster and paper scroll, selected red and blue pencils, and continued to draw on the concrete outside the window. He colored the mask and outlined the bones in blue. Hundreds of mosquitoes circled our heads and bodies, but none landed on me until I turned from the child. This sounds peculiar but he seemed to have some power over mosquitoes and other insects. Imagine a dream world where pests could be distracted with ideas and spiritual energies. Even so, I was tired of standing on the balcony and returned to the apartment.

"We were both mute on either side of the screen. I was perched inside on the wide wooden sill, and he stood near the door with one arm down, a slight stoop to the side, while mosquitoes held a spiral pattern above his head. We seemed to move at the same time, wavered together through the screen, and then it happened.

"There was a pale blue light around his head and chest, and then, much to my surprise, he grew taller right there in place. The air smelled of charcoal smoke. Crickets sounded in the room. The telephone rang and shattered the silence. The blue light burst from his head and shot from his face and arms through the screen, right through me to the telephone, like lightning to a streamer. When the light passed through me, I became the child, we became each other, and then we raised the receiver to our ear.

"I woke up then, the dream ended, but I was certain that the telephone had been ringing. The receiver was warm. I stood there in the dark with the receiver near my ear and the whole dream came back to me. Then, I was shocked

59

into the present a second time when a voice, somewhere on the other end of the line, asked me if I was alone in my room. Visitors were required to leave their names at the main desk.''

Griever dropped the telephone receiver and ran down the red carpeted stairs, three at a time, to the guest house entrance. No one was there. The windows were closed and the double doors were chained and locked. He leaned against a polished stone pedestal to catch his breath. The entrance was dark. He strained to listen over the loud sound of his heartbeat. He remembered the dream once more. The cool stone absorbed his heat. Blue light flashed across the pond. He listened until he was calm and then returned to his apartment. The door was locked, he was nude and had run out without a key.

Griever was alone in the building. He rested on the carpet at the head of the stairs like a mongrel. The loud voices of the maids awakened him at dawn. No matter how he tried to approach the maids, his crotch covered with a small carpet, or covered with newspapers, no one would open the apartment door. He waited in the corner until the foreign affairs officer arrived with the key to the door.

"Hot weather," said Egas Zhang.

"Right," said the trickster and rushed into the apartment.

"Look, telephone on floor."

"Did you call me last night?"

"Never call at night," said Egas.

"How did you know I was locked out then?"

"Maids call me," he laughed.

"Did you see a mute child last night?"

"No, not last night."

"Well, when did you see him then?"

"Yaba Gezi, the mute pigeon," Egas said at the screen

60

door to the balcony. "Child from old stories, no one sees the mute, from stories before liberation."

"Wu Chou, he saw the child, he must have seen the mute child, he sees everyone who comes through the gate," the trickster insisted. "Yaba Gezi is more than a story."

"He sees stories," said Egas.

"Who tells stories about the child?"

"Peasants," said Egas.

"This is a nation of peasants."

"Superstitious peasants."

"Like you, and for good reason."

"Old superstitious peasants," he said and blew smoke through the screen. He snorted and tapped his cheek.

"Do people tell stories about you?"

"Mister Griever," he said and stared at the trickster, a decisive voice and serious turn in the discussion, "you buy bear paw for me?"

"Bear paws?"

"Indian, you have bear paw."

"Paws or claws?"

"Paws, and gallbladder."

"Why paws?"

"Medicine," he answered. Egas continued to stare at the trickster but he moved his head from side to side like an animal. "Medicine for heart, bone, neck. . . ."

"Dick medicine," the trickster shouted and smiled.

"Elbow, ear, nose, stomach. . . ."

"Listen, bear paws you want, bear paws you get," said the trickster eager to earn a favor with the cadres in the foreign affairs bureau. "Give me a few weeks to order them from the reservation."

"Hot weather, too much hot weather." Egas smiled, stooped several times and then pulled the door closed. Out-

61

side he smoked a cigarette and listened near the door until he heard the water run in the toilet.

Griever was standing in the shower when he remembered the drawings the mute child made in his dream. He rushed to the balcony, nude and wet. There, near the door, he found the round mask and the outline of a man with small blue bones in his hands.

PART 2

DASHU: GREAT HEAT

More than the freedom to think, Chinese
intellectuals long for the freedom to believe
that truth exists. . . . In a society where for
decades intellectuals have been thwarted in
their quest for knowledge, it is no wonder
that they turn for inspiration to the defiant
Galileo. . . . No wonder, too, that they use
and misread Bertolt Brecht. . . . They are
missing, however, Brecht's message that all
truth is temporal, changeable, according to
the needs and circumstances of its
proponents and its opponents.

> VERA SCHWARCZ
> *Long Road Home: A China Journal*

The lives of the revolutionary writers in
Communist China have more importance
than their literary works. Despite the
party's determination to eliminate them as
a distinct group and to incorporate all
intellectuals into the state bureaucracy,
they were an amorphous, yet independent,
island in the vast sea of the bureaucracy.

> MERLE GOLDMAN
> *Literary Dissent in Communist China*

¶ Panic Holes

Egas Zhang, the furtive director of foreign affairs at Zhou Enlai University, held a cigarette close to his cheek, a pose revised from western movies, when he entered the dining room at the guest house. He carried a small plastic case attached to his wrist with braided twine.

"Hot time now," said Egas.

"Hot time, the weather," one teacher answered with a smile but the other teachers were suspicious. Egas approached with his hand on his cheek; his lean fingers were stained brown between the knuckles. Small collars of blue smoke broke over his hard right ear when he stooped near the head of the table and exhaled his words. His breath smelled of nicotine and spiced sausage.

"Professor Griever," he said, and pinched back his sinister smile, "please, you finished now recording language lessons?"

"Lessons, what lessons?" Griever held back his smile too, at the brow of bad humor, and looked down the table to the other teachers for their approval.

Silence.

Egas had asked most of the teachers within a few hours of their arrival at the guest house, when they were all too eager to please the cadres responsible for their appointments, their apartments, travel arrangements, their meals and mail, to record language tapes, which he duplicated and then sold to students at other institutions. He pressured the teachers to complete the tapes before the end of the second week of classes because he knew from past experience that his exotic cultural power, based on the romantic idealism of the teachers, would wear thin in less than a month.

Egas stooped even lower at the table. He was not aware that humid morning that the teachers were troubled over political events in other parts of the world.

"English lessons," said Egas. He snapped his head back and expanded his chest. "You promised to me this week the tapes, this is time now."

"Soon, real soon now," muttered Griever. He pointed out the wide windows. "Did you hear, did you hear the terrible news?"

"Whose news?" he responded and nodded his head at each teacher around the table. Eight uncommon teachers from east to west at breakfast: Griever de Hocus, the mixedblood trickster; Luther Holes, the valetudinarian and guest house sycophant; Hannah Dustan, the computer separatist; Carnegie Morgan, also known as Carnie, the tallest teacher with the widest mouth and a rich name; Gingerie Anderson-Peterson, place name consumer with a peculiar accent; Jack and Sugar Dee, the inseparable industrial management consultants; and Colin Marplot Gloome, the retired time and motion scholar. Matteo Ricci, the prime cock liberated from the market, was perched on the back of a chair.

"Please, chickens no place in guest house," said Egas. He butted his heels when he spoke, released his sinister smile, and punched his cigarette into a saucer at the end of the table. He hated chickens even more than foreigners. He stared at the cock and waited with his hands behind his back for an answer.

66

"Three hundred innocent people were murdered this morning over omelettes and croissants," the trickster shouted.

"Two hundred and sixty-nine," said Hannah Dustan.

"What's with the menu?" asked Carnegie Morgan.

"Egas Zhang," chanted Luther Holes, an obvious gesture to turn the conversation and gain his favor, "could we make an appointment to talk about my tapes later this afternoon?"

"This afternoon," the trickster mocked. "Innocent people were murdered and you talk about those damned language tapes." Griever covered his plate with a napkin.

"The last righteous bastard to come through here cracked in three months," said Luther, the one teacher who had returned for a second year. "Those tapes, if you and your rooster must know, are important to me and the development of the language skills in this country."

"That plane had nuclear bombs," blurted Colin Gloome, who lectures but never listens. "They had no business being over a missile base at night."

Voice of America radio reported that interceptors from the Soviet Union had shot down a South Korean civilian airliner that morning over the Sea of Japan near Sakhalin Island. Radio Moscow denied the report as imperialist propaganda, but later admitted that the interceptors had "fired warning shots and tracer shells along the flight route of the plane," which was on a routine flight from Anchorage, Alaska, to Kimpo Airport in Seoul when it crossed into Soviet airspace. The cabin exploded at breakfast, seven miles over the sea.

Matteo Ricci spread his sickle feathers.

Gingerie snickered.

Colin was suspicious and brushed his sleeves.

Luther was neutral to the news.

Sugar Dee wiped her tears.

Egas clicked his teeth together. He stooped once more and moved back from the aliens at the table, back to the dark kitchen with the cadres.

"Egas, the poor bastard, he took ten years to learn Russian and then the revolution turned the tables on him, Russian was out and English was in, overnight," said Carnie. "Pass the salt down here."

"Egas cares too much about his work," explained Luther. He looked around the table, eager to find an audience for his comments. "We should take the time to talk with him, to share the problems he has in running this guest house."

"Not easy, right?" mocked Carnie.

"Right."

"Hundreds of people exploded over breakfast and you talk about problems in the guest house," said Griever. His voice trembled, he pressed his hands down on the table and looked out the window, his escape distance.

Matteo Ricci beat and bounced over the table from the back of a chair to the open window. Griever turned and in three bounds he was over the window sill behind the cock. Outside, he marched around the pond behind the guest house. The cock walked with the trickster, he turned familiar stones and pecked at worms and delicate insects from the darkness.

"That man should be institutionalized," said Luther.

"Like most of us," added Carnie.

"We should do something about his foul cock," said Jack. She wrinkled her nose and groaned. "There we were, our first day at the market when he forced a merchant to dispose of his chickens, all but that rude rooster."

"We could eat the rooster," said Sugar Dee.

"That cock, however, is but one symptom of a much deeper emotional problem," Luther explained to the teach-

68

ers at the table. He sipped tea and watched the trickster on the other side of the pond.

"Holes, you're full of shit," said Carnie. He pushed his chair back to leave. "He's no crazier than you are, than any of us in this fucked place."

"Luther, you make good sense," said Gloome.

"Should we bake the cock?"

"Sugar Dee, you cook the cock," mocked Hannah.

"Listen," said Carnie from the door, "leave the cock alone and leave me out of your conspiracies." He waved his hands and slammed the dining room doors.

"What evah is that strange man doing now?" asked Gingerie. She brushed her hair back and walked to the window. "Look, thah he is down on his knees neah the pond."

"He did that the first week we arrived," explained Hannah from the end of the table. "It was dusk and I was out about to light a cigarette when I heard this terrible scream from across the pond, several screams," she said and lighted a cigarette with a golden match. She inhaled three times before she continued. "Well, I was sure there was an emergency so I ran to the guest house and managed to communicate to the fool at the desk, you would think after all this time that someone here could speak our language, he finally understood and hurried around the pond to the sound of the screams."

"Listen," said Luther, "you can hear him scream."

"Lock him up," said Gloome.

"You can hear the cock," said Sugar Dee.

"Continue out here," Luther said and then climbed outside. The other teachers crowded around the window. Gingerie brushed her hair back, Jack and Sugar Dee touched each other at the thighs and shoulders, Gloome pulled at the wild white hairs in his nostrils, and Hannah chewed on

69

a thin cigarette as she smoked and talked about the first night she heard the trickster scream.

"Well, by the time we got there it was dark," said Hannah. Her face was pale and oiled; small bales of flesh rolled under her arms and neck when she inhaled and turned her head to speak. "Over there, past that little brick house on the other side of the pond we found him down on his hands and knees, like he is now, and he was screaming into a small hole."

"Hannah," Gingerie interrupted with her pink nails raised, "do you know if the man is married? Does he have a family?"

"What difference would that make?" asked Luther.

"Well, he might miss his wife or family," she explained.

"Do you miss your husband?"

"Not really," she replied.

"Well, Gingerie is quite right," said Hannah, "my heart went out to him at first, he was strange but there was something attractive about him doubled over and screaming into a hole in the earth."

"What was he screaming about?" asked Sugar Dee.

"He didn't say."

"How did he explain his behavior?" asked Luther.

"Well, he told the man from the guest house that he screamed into a *hai pa* hole to balance the world, or something like that."

"Hannah, what does that mean?"

"*Hai pa* means 'fear,'" said Luther.

"The little man seemed to understand and the two of them laughed all the way back to the guest house, while I stumbled after them in the dark," said Hannah. "They seemed to forget I was there, but later, much later, he told me that he had little holes all over the place where he screamed, at least twice a week." She paused to light another cigarette and then continued. "He called them panic

70

holes, and he said he has buried his voice around the world in panic gardens."

"Look, now he covers his hole," said Jack.

"Like an animal," said Sugar Dee.

"He's wonderful," said Gingerie, "now I know what he was doing when I found him planting a little tree in a hole, he plants something in his panic holes."

"Griever told me that he buried his rage in those panic holes to protect the people he loves," explained Hannah.

"Such a nice man," said Gingerie.

"Propaganda," said Gloome.

"He trusted me," said Hannah. She was attracted to what she thought were weaknesses in the trickster, and she was not at ease with the other women.

Gingerie brushed her hair back and watched the trickster and his cock circle back to the guest house. She waited at the window and waved to him when he passed. Matteo Ricci spread his sickle feathers and shook his wattles.

¶ Stone Shaman

Shitou breaks stones with one hand late in the afternoon three times a week at the entrance to the free market in a close near the campus gate. Between the breaks he tells stories about bears and the old stone cultures that came down from the mountains and settled near the sea.

"Shitou is a stone," he declared each time he danced around the stones, his ritual preparation for the break. "Smiles break, blue water breaks, birds break in a storm, children break, minds and hearts break," he chanted to the small crowd, "and this old hand breaks stones into laughter."

Li Wen, a student from the language institute, translated the rituals of the stone man. She had approached the trickster earlier to practice casual conversation.

Several people turned their faces down, others raised their shoulders closer to their ears, and some men rocked their heads with laughter when the old stone man raised his venerable hand above the stones. There were few women in the crowd; the men and children there seemed more desperate, either to discommend the simple rituals, or to believe in the spiritual power of the stone and the humor in the breaks.

Griever was there, mettlesome, proud to be a mixed-blood trickster and related to the stone in his own tribal

72

origin stories. He watched the old stone man from behind two soldiers dressed in common uniforms: oversized blue trousers, olive coats with brown leather belts, and authentic red stars on the front of their caps. The men smoked thin brown cigarettes and laughed at the stories.

"Shitou is a stone. . . ."

Griever asked Li Wen to translate what the soldiers had said about the stone man. The student seemed hesitant to reveal what she had heard.

"Shitou is a monkey, the soldiers with scar said monkey," she translated. Li Wen moved closer to the trickster, unsure and uncomfortable, and whispered near his ear. Her hair, set in small curls, tickled his cheek. The curls were unusual in a nation that viewed vanities and cosmetics as a form of spiritual pollution. He discovered later that she wore wigs, one with real hair from the head of her grandmother and another curled from black plastic. She wore real hair at special events and her plastic curls to college classes.

"Monkeys learned how to break," she continued to whisper her translation to the trickster, "when to break, stones for foreign missionaries."

Shitou placed the smooth river boulders on a low bench that was attached to the back of his three-wheeler; and then, with his right hand, he cracked them down to slivers and shards. The soldiers rocked with derisive laughter.

Shitou stood over the breaks and inhaled the breath of bears sealed in the stones. He was short and stooped with rounded shoulders. The muscles on his lower back were limber, and when he raised his arms he seemed much taller than five feet. Even so, he was shorter than most of the children in the circle. His arms were stretched from hard labor in the stone mines and his hands, at rest, touched his knees.

The shape of his bald head, his wide ears, and funnel

73

chest, cast him closer to an anurous simian than a bear or a stone. His chest was bare; smooth muscles flounced like water animals when he raised a stone. Loose blue trousers were tucked under a wide canvas belt tied tight around his waist. The black cloth shoes he wore were faded and threadbare over his broad toes. The stories he told about the old stone cultures, and the heat that flashed from his one good eye, separated him from the experiences of the audience and from the tame public images of socialism.

Matteo Ricci crowed over the stones.

Shitou was alone; his wife and three children died near the end of the revolution. To break stones at the market with his bare hands with no collective purpose, to entertain tourists, and to receive gratuities were not considered pertinent service to the new state; moreover, the cadres would not provide medical care or housing for the old man because he did not have a permanent work place.

"Shitou is a stone," he recited once more and then loaded the stone breaks into a wooden box. He collected the few coins and bills from a small wicker basket and tied these presents into a small cloth bundle which he tucked under his canvas belt. He took less from others and earned more through his imagination in three afternoons a week than the state could provide in a whole month.

The sun, down close to the trees, burned behind his wide thin ears and touched his clouded right eye. The old stone face creased like bark when he smiled; his lower teeth were short, blunt, stained, and his right eyelid drooped closed. His motions and appearance reminded the trickster of the old shamans on the reservation.

Shitou mounted his three-wheeler with the rusted chain and pedaled in a circle around the close, his ritual departure. The sun dropped behind the campus gate when he passed.

"Shitou is a broken monkey," the soldiers shouted.

74

"Shitou is a stone," the trickster muttered several times. He raised his small hands behind the soldiers and cracked them hard on the shoulders. The men were stunned, weakened on one side, and when the soldiers turned, the trickster snickered and shadowboxed around their heads. The men ducked and moved to the side, out of reach.

"*Wai guo ren,*" one soldier shouted.

"*Yang gui zi,*" said the soldier with the scar.

"What did they say?" Griever asked the student who had moved to the other side of the circle. Li Wen smiled but she would not translate their denunciation.

"An external person," said Luther Holes from the outside of the circle, "a foreigner." Holes and Hannah Dustan had been at the free market in search of bananas.

"*Yang gui zi* means 'foreign devil,'" added Hannah. "That was the first phrase we learned to prepare us for this place." She touched a red brooch over her right breast when she spoke; she was a high fashion computer dealer with a resonant voice. Her face, arms, and shoulders were blotched with dark pigmentation from sunburns. Pale puckers on her cheeks and below her ears gathered, and then trailed down her neck to her thickset ankles. The puckers opened and closed when she walked and talked.

Hannah wore a loose peach colored blouse that revealed the mass of her low breasts from the side, through the wide sleeves. Several bracelets and ornamental chains rattled on her wrists when she conducted each spoken word with a shoulder, arm, and mad hand gesture. Most people watched her first and listened later; indeed, she was asked to repeat words, sentences, even whole paragraphs, in casual conversations. The trickster watched her and remembered the social workers on the reservation.

"Can you believe all this?" she asked.

"What was that?" asked Griever.

"This, all of this," she gestured to the crowd.

75

"The stone shaman."

"Who would believe this?" She waved her hands and looked around the close near the free market. Women sauntered through the intersection with white gloves and plastic shoes; some wheeled their green bicycles, with the saddles set too high, through the crowds. Men frowned in white shirts and smoked short cigarettes. Children wore bright colored clothes and watched the blue carp swim past on the street.

"Pigs in bicycle baskets, and dead ones stacked on the corner over there," she said and pointed in several directions. "Chickens butchered right on the street, filth everywhere, high and low, and in the middle of it all, here we are watching this pathetic parade while some old clown breaks his hand on rocks for a few pennies."

"Some people break their ass for nothing," said Griever.

"Where?"

"White Earth, even in San Francisco."

"Look at that," she shouted and pointed to a small truck overloaded with baskets of fresh vegetables. An adolescent with a straw peasant hat and blue sunglasses was perched on the back with a cassette recorder on his shoulder. "Do my ears deceive me?" She cocked her head to listen as the truck passed. "Christmas music? Jesus Christ, can you believe it? 'Jingle Bells,' here, in the middle of summer, 'dashing through the snow,' this is either the start of a new revolution or the end of the goddamn world."

Hannah raised her arms and snapped her fingers to the music. She pretended to be casual, to be open and humorous, but she cleared her throat too much. The soldiers leaned even closer, one on each side, to watch her breasts bounce beneath the wide sleeves. Chinese men seldom have the pleasure to behold a huge bourgeois breast, the ultimate in spiritual pollution.

"Shitou is a stone," whispered Griever.

"Even a stone is not that simple," said Hannah. The shallow color drained from her cheeks; she tapped a tune on her front teeth with one plastic fingernail. The animation of her mouth and her hands slackens when she remembers two recurrent dreams. In the first, she is haunted by dark children who claim she is their mother; in the second, columns of silent immigrants stand in public welfare lines around her house, and when she tries to enter, hundreds of hands touch her clothes and examine the labels and seams. In both dreams, the children and immigrants are mixedbloods, their hands soiled and covered with mold.

Hannah and her third husband, who is president of the San Clemente College of Butlers and Maidservants, could not find the time to travel because of a new demand for menials. She is a hereditist, withstands miscegenation, and neither speaks nor listens to people that she determines are mixedbloods. More than once she has turned in silence from a conversation when she discovered that the person was a mixture of races. She did not know about the racial identities of the trickster.

Hannah, however, does not celebrate her racial insecurities at random; indeed, her racialism is formal and methodological. For example, she is hostile to miscegenation because she believes that mixedbloods are inferior. "Mix oil and water and you end up with neither," she argues, but her metaphors are seldom as persuasive as her research summaries; her racialist bone of contention is based on distorted demographic information. "Chinese, now take these people here, victims the world over, but not so much as their mixedblood children," she explained to several new teachers on the train. "Even so, when people can be recognized for what they are, then they do better in the world. Jews, like the Chinese and other races, achieve more and earn more in those countries where there is discrimination, but not mixedbloods because no one knows who they are.

77

Mixedbloods are neither here nor there, not like real bloods." Hannah cleared her throat and tapped her teeth with a fingernail.

"Brown fingernails, are those real?" asked Griever.

"These people are still learning how to dress themselves and we are supposed to teach them how to use computers," said Hannah. She raised one hand to summon her driver. He drove the car over the sidewalk and parked on the close. The soldiers scurried to open the rear door of the black limousine. When she leaned over to the back seat, the men saw her breasts tumble one last time. She waved with one hand from behind the brown curtains as the driver honked the loud horn several times and roared between two trucks.

"How does she rate a chauffeur?" asked Griever.

"Microcomputers," answered Holes.

"Computers?"

"First there were plastics and now the password is *dian nao*, electric brain, the computer," he said, envious and disappointed. "Name that computer and win a ride in a limousine." Holes had returned to teach a second year, with no commendation from the cadres, and now a common computer dealer had neglected to offer him a ride back to the guest house.

"Too much dust here to run computers," said Griever.

"Like the people," Luther muttered.

Griever waited at the intersection near the free market. He looked down both sides of the street and then walked in the same direction as the stone man had pedaled. Buses howled, horns honked, horses languored at the curb. The trickster pinched his ear and searched for a wild hair.

ℊ Black Opal

Griever bucked to the head of the line at the main bus stop near the train station. He touched shoulders, thighs, enravished with moist bodies in the crush; such sensuous pleasures were denied in other public places.

The trickster was urbane in the classroom; he paused at some social intersections and at the thresholds of past rulers, but he could bear insipid manners no more than a few weeks. The people who crushed each other on the run seldom touched with esteem when there was time. Machines, the trickster noted, were parked much closer than lovers were allowed to be seen. The teachers in the guest house tolerated his stories about unusual events on the streets, but dismissed his intimations on cold cultures and the wiles of socialist bureaucracies.

"Now there, my friends, is a real paranoid man," said Luther Holes when the trickster was out of the room. "There's no give in him, he hits the streets like a milk bottle, tumbles down the stairs and breaks on the last step."

"Nevah, Grievah is the one who remembahs his friends caught in thundahstorms with no umbrellas." Gingerie enunciated each word in isolation, as if she were recording the moment in a high school graduation annual.

Griever was content once to take his time at the turnstiles, rather pleased to cede his independence to the casual order of the line and to tattle with the others there, but not here in the middle land; when he waited on manners here he lost his place and missed the bus.

Chinese men shaved their scant mortalities from public lines and pushed past children and old women loaded with bundles, baskets, live chickens, and without apologies, not even an artless salute. The trickster watched, then he practiced, and in time he rivaled their strategies and public moves; he outwitted the local men, even soldiers on the streets, in the hard brush. He lost interest in the best seats on the bus, but his impulse to touch bodies in the public press never waned. Behind these cultural masks, in the guest house, at banquets and special social events, the trickster bucked the lines in conversations as he would to touch bodies in the terminal crowds.

The double doors on the diesel bus cracked closed, one more social implosion that could have crushed a slow arm, a hesitant head or chest. The driver, a small woman with muscular calves and thighs, cut the engine at each stop to conserve fuel. She would be honored by the transportation cadres, saved two gallons of fuel that month; no matter that the bus died four times and had to be towed back to the station. Loaded, the engine was slow to start; it turned over several times, coughed, clanked, and the windows shuddered. The bus was crowded, hot, and smelled of garlic and fine brown dust from a construction site.

The trickster was pinched between two old women, each with a small cloth bundle, and a row of seats in the middle of the tandem bus. He held his head back, pretended to breathe the air from a narrow vent over the aisle. The old women carried the scent of cabbages, wet chicken feathers, and charcoal smoke.

The bus shuddered once more and then lurched from the curb into traffic. The wheels rumbled down the rough road, each tire a coarse sensor over the narrow cracks and seams in the concrete and asphalt pavement laid since the revolution.

Griever pinched and folded his right ear.

Victoria Park, the old name in colonial concessions, wavered when the bus turned. The park was contorted behind the narrow windows; seasons twisted, and the trees were warped at the corner. Wild blooms, children, and palmar birds were broken in motion; and familiar faces on the street undulated on a shallow pool. The trickster watched other worlds through the overhead vent; the broad leaves that covered the old concessions and the memories of the colonists.

The ceremonies commenced when the Royal Artillery and Welsh Fusiliers marched to the bandstand in Victoria Park. Then the American band arrived and an audience gathered to hear sacred music. The French, Russian, American, and British soldiers and sailors, and numerous concession officials, sang "Shall we gather at the river," with Bishop Scott and the pastoral staff. The Boxers, harmonious fists, also gathered at the river, the Hai He.

Herbert Hoover, a mining engineer, and his wife Lou Henry Hoover took cover in the Foreign Settlement near Victoria Park in Tianjin. "In hunting material for barricades," he wrote, "we lit upon the great godowns filled with sacked sugar, peanuts, rice and other grains. . . . The big attack came the second day, but the marines and sailors repulsed it from behind our bags."

The bus stopped at the far corner of the park. The double doors opened like a theater curtain on a woman whose wide face was painted with bright colors, and who wore a red silk coat embroidered on the collar and sleeves. She appeared to be a character from the classical opera, stranded in the park; she stood at the doors, composed in a scene, but would not board the bus. "Save this park," she said and

81

waved a horsehair duster at the driver and conductor; the robust sound of those three words bounced inside the bus.

Griever moved closer to the door to answer the woman but a man with a golden water bottle and a string bag filled with green pears blocked the aisle. The man had vacated the seat in front of two old women. When he turned to leave the bus, two pears dropped through the mesh and bounced on the metal floor. One old woman, she wore a blue shirt with a high collar, captured both pears. The man smiled, his front teeth were broken, and then he leaped from the bus with a pear in each hand. He hit the street so hard that one foot shot through the end of a plastic sandal. He hopped from the bus with one sandal around his ankle, past the woman with the painted face. She did not seem to notice the man, the sandal, or the pears. She waved the horsehair duster at the windows and then disappeared behind the trees in the park.

The doors cracked closed and the engine rumbled on the second turn of the starter. The two old women watched the man with the pears through the warped window. One woman held back a smile; the other woman laughed in whispers and covered her mouth with one hand. Most of her teeth were gone; when she spoke her lips puckered like a goldfish at the surface of a pond. On the middle finger of her right hand she wore a wide gold band and a black opal surrounded with faceted blue stones, rare lapis lazuli and blue garnets. The opal burned on her short stout finger, out of place on the crowded bus; a present from a rich relative who had escaped the revolution. The stones shimmered, red palmations on her cheeks, ancient tribal fires in the silica beads, blue and green. She wore black cloth shoes, a peasant with wide toes; her shoulders were drawn inward on a narrow chest. This precious opalescence transformed her time on the bus down London Meadows, the old concessions road.

Griever was slow to remember his dream about the murals in the Kingdom of Khotan and the fire bear who wore the same black opal and lapis lazuli; but when he did remember he unholstered his scroll so the old woman could see the bright stones he had drawn from a dream scene.

"Listen, where did you find that ring?" Griever touched the old woman on the elbow; he gestured with his mouth and hands, an invitation to take the one vacant seat on the bus.

"*Jue bu,* 'never,'" she said and covered her mouth with one hand. The old woman snickered, insisted that the trickster take the seat. The black opal blazed on her cheeks. He reversed the common realities and pushed the woman down on the vacant seat. She resisted; the trickster held her down with his hand on her shoulder.

"Mister Griever, please, you remember me from last time?" asked the student who had translated at the stone breaks.

"Li Wen," he said and held out his hands.

"You do remember."

"But your hair is different."

"Perhaps my hair was curled last time." She did not tell the trickster that she was bald and that she used two wigs, one with curls and the other with a braid.

"Yes, the curls," responded Griever. He moved closer and held the thick braid in one hand; he touched each turn in the plait. She was embarrassed and wanted to tell him that the hair was from her grandmother.

"You need directions?" asked Li Wen.

"No, but could you ask that woman over there where she found that opal and the blue stones," said the trickster.

"She does not answer."

"That ring was in my dreams," he said and held his balance. The bus rumbled over broken concrete on the road. "Tell her that a fire bear wore that opal on the old silk road."

"She does not answer."

"She must, that was my dream, tell her again."

"No, she will not answer."

"What did you say?"

"Have you visited the market?"

"Li Wen, please ask her if the opal is for sale."

"She does not answer now."

"Why not?"

"Have you visited the market?"

"Incredible, the cultural tolerance for repetition."

"Yes, thank you very much," said Li Wen.

"Listen, do you know where the old stone man lives?" asked the trickster. The bus stopped at a hospital; the new passengers smelled of alcohol and antiseptic vapors.

"He breaks stones three times a week," she said and avoided his question. She reached for the overhead support bar when the bus turned near the language institute. The outline of her small breasts, and enormous black nipples, were pressed beneath her white blouse, drawn tight when she extended her arm. "This is my stop."

"Do you live near here?"

"We live and study at the language institute," she explained with a generous smile and then she turned toward the side doors. The old women studied her moves, head to waist, and then stared at her plastic shoes. Her toes were small and unblemished, nails trimmed, clear, and polished.

"Wait, please wait," he pleaded.

"This bus stops at the college," she reassured the trickster with a gentle voice. "Watch for the canal and then you must get down at the next stop."

"Do you know where to find the stone man?" Griever repeated his question until the doors closed and the bus

84

moved back into traffic. Li Wen missed the stop at the language institute.

"Near the end of the canal," she answered.

"Could you show me?"

"We are not allowed to travel there," she explained and looked around the bus to see who had heard her speak. She pressed closer to the door, prepared to leave at the next stop.

"Not allowed?"

"The soldiers are there."

"What?"

"Forbidden," she whispered closer to his ear. He could feel the heat from her cheeks. "Not good to be with foreigners there, no travel there."

"Pretend then."

"Not pretend," she said, "we are not the same as you, we cannot visit the same places without special reason, some places are forbidden."

"Shitou is the reason," he insisted.

"Not reason." She was nervous, distracted, and excited at the same time, with nothing more than a simple invitation to be seen in public with a foreign teacher. Her thighs were moist with perspiration. "You do not understand," she said and covered her mouth with one hand.

Griever smiled and pleaded with her to direct him to the house of the old stone man. She resisted and turned toward the double doors.

Meanwhile, the trickster maneuvered behind the second old woman and pushed her down into the last vacant seat; she bounced back up and he pushed her down a second time and held her there. The woman was not pleased; she lectured the trickster with a maternal tone of voice. The others on the crowded bus were amused by what the woman said to the foreigner.

"What did she say to me?"   85

"Nothing," said Li Wen.

"Tell them that a man in my country would be ashamed to take a seat from an old woman," said the trickster. He looked around at the faces on the bus. People watched him from a cultural distance, but their laughter was not unkind. Several children stared at his outsized nose.

"Tell them their culture needs a twist when the men get the best seats and the old women must stand," he shouted.

"Twist, what does that mean?"

"Confucius would give his seat to an old woman," he insisted. "Communist cadres, on the other hand, took the best seats and called it a cultural revolution."

Li Wen translated part of what the trickster had said, but nothing about the cadres. She attributed his impetuous speech to the insecurities of capitalism. The two old women chattered in their seats.

"What are they saying now?"

"They said you are a monkey king."

"Tell them this," he insisted with a mischievous smile, "tell them that even foreign monkeys never cheat old women from their seats on the bus."

Trained to be a polite translator, she listened to the trickster and missed the second bus stop, one past the language institute where she lived. Li Wen translated most of what the trickster said; the old women listened with their cloth bundles on their knees.

"Now, this must be my stop, must leave, must leave," she said as the bus shuddered and stopped once more. "No more to translate now."

"Wait," said the trickster. He moved between her and the double doors, unaware that he had stepped on her toes. "We are close to the university, we could eat at the guest house, then we could walk down the canal and search for the stone man."

"We are not allowed to do such things," she whispered

86

over the pain in her toes. Her hands trembled when she spoke. "I am a student and you are a foreign teacher."

"Foreign, indeed," he mocked.

"You find stone man."

"But we need a translator," he insisted, "we need you to translate the old stone stories, and to keep me company."

"Shitou speaks English," said Li Wen.

"He doesn't."

"Yes, he does, he once lived in the United States."

"He did?"

"Yes," she answered.

When the bus stopped and the double doors opened the two old women bounced from the seat, turned, and with unusual balance, pushed the trickster backward into the seat. They held him down and laughed; others on the bus pointed their fingers and laughed too, and then the two women hurried from the bus. The doors cracked closed and the student stood with the two women and waved at the trickster. Their hands were twisted behind the uneven window pane, the blue stones and the opal blazed from a distance.

❡ Peach Emperor

Matteo Ricci thrust his head from the canvas shoulder pack and clucked at the teachers in line at the train station. When the trickster saw the woman with the scar and the blue rabbit, the woman he had pursued at the bus stop near the campus, he rushed the lines to the turnstiles.

"Remember me?"

"You are the foreign teacher," she responded. Muscles on her neck tightened, and with each word the volume of her voice increased. She was carried with the crowd through the turnstile.

"Call me Griever," he cried and hied with the blue press to the train. Women and children heard the cock and waited at the side of the line. "Wait, wait, who are you?"

"Hester Hua Dan."

"Hester?"

"Yes, yes, the translator for teacher tour," she said. When she smiled, the carinal scar held one cheek down while the other spread back to reveal the side of her wide tongue.

"What tour are you talking about?"

"Your tour, not to worry."

"Where did you learn to talk like that?"

"Sometimes from my sister," she answered and then

turned to direct the other teachers to the proper coach and their reserved seats on the train.

"Hester is an unusual name."

"We choose names to be translators."

"Marvelous," he bellowed and then whistled down the platform to the coach. The sun shivered on the horizon and burst through the windows in warehouses behind the station. Matteo Ricci crowed at the sunrise.

Griever wrote to China Browne: "Revolutions aside, this is a beautiful old colonial resort on the Gulf of Bohai north of Tangshan where thousands died in an earthquake—we could still see some of the rubble near the new train station.

"Tianjin is a wilted dandelion compared to Beidaihe where Mao Zedong vacationed. The air is fantastic here, one breath and colors are restored. Egas Zhang, the director of the foreign affairs bureau, organized this weekend for the teachers and he even provided a translator.

"The train choked, they still use steam engines, through industrial pollution for several hours while most of us slept and then when we arrived here the colors were vibrant, flowers everywhere, and the air was sweet and clean. This place is for me. Even the beach is clean, no fastfood, but then this is still a socialist state where plastic food and elevator music is high camp, and few people have permission to travel.

"The tourist brochure is too large to send and too much trouble because to mail anything larger than a letter requires a postal inspection and the lines are too long. So, here are a few lines for laughs: 'There are soft sand, a calm sea and green trees in a line.' The censors of this letter should take comfort that even the trees are in line.

"The Beidaihe resort, the brochure claims, 'Can be used to hold international or internal specialized meetings. . . .

One may take the interest of bathing in the sea or hiking over the hills in the daytime, take a stroll along the seashore to pick up shells or fish with a hook and line in the morning and evening, enjoy listening to the harmonic sounds of the soughing of the wind in the pines and the lapping of the sea at night. . . . One can feel carefree and joyous and his thoughts thronging his mind by viewing the scenic spots. . . . Foreign tourists can go camping and do self-cooking in the shade of the seaside sandy beach. . . . These are nice places for amusements by tourists.' We ate, howled at the moon, ate, built sand castles, and ate."

Colin Gloome was the last to board and locate his seat; the other teachers avoided him, so he settled with a nervous cadre and two army officers on the aisle at the back of the coach.

"Where were you during the war?" Gloome thrust his chin forward when he spoke and tightened his chest and cheeks to summon his martial memories, but no one responded. "I said, were you ever in combat, on the line?" His brows were raised to attention and he leaned toward the officers who smoked and smiled in silence.

"What war?" asked the cadre in the blue tailored tunic and oversized trousers. He wrung his hands when he translated.

"The Japs."

"That was long time before our revolution," he responded and then translated for the two officers. Clouds of blue cigarette smoke billowed from the seats. "Officers in Korean, war with Americans, no Japanese."

"Missed that one, losers down the line." Gloome leaned back in his seat and moaned; when he loosened the muscles on his chin and cheeks, the skin slid below the bone. "Listen, do you know where a man can get a face lift?"

"Face lit?"

"Lift, lift is the word," he said and pinched the flesh under his chin. "This, a face lift, a surgeon, do you have plastic surgeons over here?"

"Yes, yes, in Beijing."

"Where?"

"Maxim's de Beijing, backdoor," said the nervous cadre, and then he printed an address on the corner of an envelope. "Make new eyes, change nose here too, at this place."

"Gloome, aroint thee," the trickster ordained as he roamed in conversations. He beckoned his audience down the aisle of the coach and borrowed names and catchwords from behind smiles, pollen from the wisteria in his memories, and brandished his verbs in stories and catechisms; he interred the wild megrims in cultural histories, rained and snowed and sunned in sermons, but the mutations of his bear shadows over the couplers behind the door received mean notices from the teachers spread on their upholstered seats.

Hester Hua Dan, however, captured his moves, the clever pace of his hands as he steadied his course down the aisle. She was wakened to his trail to the rear coaches where he told stories to the lower classes crowded on the hard seats. The stories were intended for her, but the trickster foraged the courtesies of the audience, rowed over the universal gestures he could remember, and pinched his fare from spare bundles of rice and steamed vegetables to disguise the trail. Hester, warmed to his side, translated his imagined existence, fantastic episodes, and the wild pitch of the mind monkey.

"Griever de Hocus is my whole name and the stone bears collared me once on the old silk roads," the trickster told a lonesome woman who leaned too close to the window, "because, and this is the truth, my mother practiced griever meditation which allowed the fruits and vegetables to grow because the lonesome rain came to the plain."

91

The woman, who had shards of coral and cobs of turquoise braided in her hair, watched his wild gestures reflected on the window; his ears moved, and his enormous nose rutted the private gardens and the new trees spread in even rows between hamlets, but she was tribal and did not understand what she heard in translation.

Griever was determined to mind the attention of the world, even the miniature cast on the rails, but that morning he told his stories for the pleasure of the translator. She had been ransacked in his memories from one laconic encounter, and now she listened to his turns in two languages; there was no need to twist his hair to transform his time on the train.

"Bears are aroused by griever meditation," he continued in short bursts of enthusiasm, "even the old stone bears move deeper in our pockets and lumber out from the back of the closet in our old clothes. . . ."

"Wait, please," Hester pleaded from the aisle, "does stone bear mean hole in the pocket?" She watched his hands turn and tumble and touch his ears when he spoke; when he listened she was nervous because he moved closer to her side, touched her wrist once, and then her collarbone.

"The bogey bears," he bellowed to his image on the pane, "the spirit bears, the stone shaman bears, and the wild wind bears on the windows."

The train lurched to the right on a curve and he pawed one moist breast and the curve of her stomach when he leaned to hold his balance. The tribal woman with the coral and turquoise in her hair shivered on the pane. Ghost lights wavered on the brick walls and broke loose on the curve. She heard the trickster shout from the mountains and when he rolled his bear shoulders, she turned to answer, but he had moved his stories to the other end of the coach.

"The movies we saw were in our heads deep in the woods on the reservation," the trickster told a vegetable farmer, his wife, and two children, stashed on a narrow hard bench. The trickster scratched the side of his shoulder pack and Matteo Ricci thrust his head out and crowed twice. Hester translated more than he said: she told the children that he was a teacher and a clown with the humor of a mind monkey. She rendered his metaphors with imagination as she had been taught at the language institute, but descriptive names presented a cultural problem.

"Mouse Proof Martin and me fashioned a theater in the cedar trees down on the shore of Bad Medicine," he rambled hand over hand in the aisle. "Mouse Proof touched his name on the metal pedals of a bellows organ, the first words he learned to write at a reservation boarding school," said the trickster. "He had the catchies as an actor and howled when he walked, scared the shit out of the little kids and the oldies who worried about ghosts.

"We carved animal and bird figures from luminous punk and stashed them around the outdoor theater, and then," he said with his hands raised to wonder, "smile, your breasts remember me, translate that, and then we became luminous bears and wheeled through the trees and liberated the animals and birds. . . ."

"Monkey liberation," she whispered, and the more she heard the more she translated from the traditional stories of the monkey king.

"We counted the free birds," he said and leaned closer to her shoulder. Hester strained to translate while he turned her hands and drew a crude ideogram for the word monkey on her moist palm. The children laughed and he drew ideograms on their hands too, but the farmer, in a superstitious rash, spat on the characters and rubbed them clean.

Hester explained that the farmer would never let his children bear the marks of stories told by a foreign devil.

She licked the character from her hands and atoned for the teacher, one more formal practice she had learned at the language institute.

Griever mocked the children, covered his mouth with his hands, snickered and shrugged his shoulders, and then leaped down the aisle and disappeared in the toilet at the end of the coach.

Hester returned to her seat; she retreated to the window to be alone, but the other teachers pursued her to ask about the revolution, agricultural practices, abortions down on the farm, earthquakes, and classical literature, the examinations she had been trained to foresee as a translator. Griever, she was pleased to contrast between recitations, did not ask patent questions; the trickster enlivened her memories at the window. Four teachers, however, veered from the usual pattern of tourist inquiries. Gloome wanted to know more about plastic surgeons; Jack and Sugar Dee continued their search for information about lesbianism in socialist states; Carnegie, on the other hand, proposed a heterosexual union with the translator.

"Chinese culture is very old and the stories are uncertain," Hester said with a smile when she was insecure. "Our new leaders have studied these problems and will report on them soon."

"Soon is not enough," said Carnie, "I want a real date now, not some political dissertation on the future." He stood in the aisle with his huge hands buried in his pockets and pretended to kowtow. "Chinese culture, very, very old, indeed."

"Where are the best plastic surgeons?"

"Mister Gloome," she said and moved from the window to the aisle, "we are a new nation, our leaders will report on surgeons soon."

Griever crouched like a water strider on the coupler plates between the coaches, one foot in each class. He watched her move down the tunnel in the shadows: the white clench of her toes, the curve of her shins, luminous thighs wide to hold her balance, limber shoulders, and the rise of her dark moist nipples. The wheels cracked between the coaches and perspiration shivered down the scar on her cheek. He touched her moves at the bough, once, twice, and then the underside of her arm; he won her narrow waist, inhaled her breath, and rowed his tongue down the whole course of that smooth scar.

"Mister Griever," she whispered.

"Hester Hua Dan, the flower maiden."

"Names from the opera."

"Two names, Wu Chou and Hua Dan," he said and moved his hand down her back and over the waistband on her dress, "the warrior clown and the flower maiden." When she turned to block his hand, he moved his knee between her thighs; she turned once more and then leaned closer, her cheek on his chest.

"Griever, have you no shame?" Gloome, the marplot true to his name, leered and snapped his swollen knuckles. The train lurched, he lost his balance, stumbled, and hit his head on the side of the door. Hester reached to comfort him but he resisted her moves and asked for directions to the toilet.

"There, at the end of the coach."

"No, no, not the squat toilet, I want the real one with a proper seat and paper," he sneered. "Do you have toilet paper in this country?"

"Well, our leaders will report on that soon," the trick-ster mocked and then he crouched on the coupler, roared, and rolled his bear shoulders.

"Paper at other end," she said and pointed.

"Gloome, you are the prima donna of the alimentary canals," said the trickster. "You got a mouth big enough to wipe every ass on the train, no shit."

"Mongrel swine," Gloome muttered and lost his balance.

"Tangshan, Tangshan," the voice rasped over the loudspeaker, and the train pounded and screeched into the new terminal where nine years earlier more than three-hundred thousand people had died in an earthquake.

Griever clenched his teeth, covered his ears, and waited for the train to stop. Hester was timid now, suspicious that the trickster had been insincere. He smiled, raised both hands and opened one to reveal four ideograms painted on his palm; the characters for the words love, house, extend, and monkey, were borrowed from a traditional proverb which he modified for the moment. He substituted the monkey ideogram for the crow, which means, in translation, "If you love a house, you love its monkey."

Hester covered her mouth and turned to leave the train at the station when the trickster flashed four more ideograms on his right hand: plant, melon, gain, and a second melon, which means in translation, "If you plant melons, you reap melons." She burst into wild laughter over the proverbs and the peculiar presentation of the mind monkey; he raised his hands, flashed the characters several times; she held her stomach, doubled over between the coaches.

"If you touch vermilion, you get stained red," she said over her shoulder, "if you touch ink you get stained black."

"Stain me red. . . ."

"What do you get when you touch a mind monkey?"

"Toilet paper," he shouted and followed her into the crowd at the terminal. She vanished in a marble of blue trousers and white shirts.

"Tangshan is much too modern," Griever wrote to China Browne, "new concrete buildings reinforced with steel beams stand in even rows, and this newness is a constant reminder that hundreds of thousands of people died here in less than a minute. Even so, there was still a blue horde at the station where we stopped for a few minutes. While we were there I bought an official government bulletin about the earthquake, which happened on July 28, 1976, and the reconstruction. 'The quake lasted for twenty-three seconds, but the destruction it caused to lives and property was unparalleled in modern world history. . . . You can still see the vestiges of the earthquake in the narrow side streets full of rubble. Half the inhabitants are still living in small brick houses roofed with asphalt felt weighted down with bricks. . . .' Sounds like a reservation back home, minus the bricks."

"Listen to this," he said to the other teachers as the train, bound for the resort, cleared the terminal. Griever read from the bulletin as rows of new apartment buildings moved past the windows:

"Tangshan people, who have tested their mettle against death, are now plunged into a battle to return their shattered city to its former self and get their lives rolling anew," he read, and then commented that their civilization might have ended with a little harder shake of the earth.

"Is this where the turtles screamed?" asked Gingerie.

"What turtles?"

"Tangshan Little League," said Carnie.

"Miss Gingerie means that turtles scream when earthquake comes," explained Hester. "Our leaders studied the turtles and no turtles screamed here."

"Turtles never scream," insisted Sugar Dee.

"They got married in 1977, she a 35-year-old teacher of the Tangshan branch of the China Coal-Mining Research Institute and he one of the branch's assistant engineers," the trickster continued to read as the train shuddered over

97

rougher rails. "Both lost their spouses the night the quake ravaged the city and each was left with a child.

"But it took a while to get their marriage going. At first, the wife was unhappy about her stepdaughter, who kept her at arm's length."

"Can the rest, Griever," carped Hannah.

"Nevah, nevah, read more."

"The new earthquake soaps," said Luther.

"Read, read," pleaded Sugar Dee.

"She remembered once taking the little girl to watch television away from home," he continued from the aisle, "but a meeting was going on in the television room, and they had to go home, disappointed."

"Chinese child abuse," mocked Carnie.

"The girl thought her stepmother did not really mean to let her watch television and cried: 'You're not my mom, leave me alone.' The woman was hurt and wept," the trickster moaned with commiseration. "She knew it would be difficult to give the child enough affection to console her for the loss of her mother. Still she tried. . . .

"Petty bickering occasionally broke out between husband and wife, but all helped, one way or another, to deepen their love. One morning, the daughter dilly-dallied for too long and was late for school. The mother scolded her, but the father seemed not to take this seriously, saying to his daughter, 'Don't you worry, I'll see you to school if you are late.' This embarrassed the wife and she retorted, 'We are of two families after all, from now on, I won't say anything about your daughter.'

"At these words, the husband angrily stormed away to work," the trickster read, pinched his ear, and then he smiled, "without eating breakfast."

"Poor little man," said Jack.

"Now hold it down, Jack," warned Carnie.

"Lesbians are never insincere," muttered Hannah.

98

"Read, read," pleaded Sugar Dee.

"The wife, fearing that he might suffer from his stomach trouble, boiled milk with egg. 'As I hurried to catch up with him, I bumped into him on his way back. He was sorry about the argument and was returning to see if I was all right. This really brought us closer.'

"They are but one of the hundred couples at the Tangshan branch of the China Coal-Mining Research Institute who rebuilt their families after their husbands or wives died in the quake," the trickster read. When the train whistle sounded, he paused to wave at the peasants stooped at a crossroad with their enormous bales.

"Peasants no more," shouted Gloome. He spread his wrinkled hands on the pane. "Look, one of them has a new television set strapped to the back of his bicycle."

"*Tableau vivant*," sighed Hannah.

"The branch's trade union staff, who have volunteered to be matchmakers," he continued to read from the bulletin when the peasants had faded in the distance, "are now racking their brains to find mates for the remaining three widowers and six widows. . . .

"The nightmarish earthquake left twenty-six hundred orphan children. Some seven hundred of them have been sent to schools in Shijiazhuang and Xingtai. . . . The rest have been adopted either by relatives or sympathizers."

"Where is that?"

"Tangshan in same province," said Hester.

"The school in Shijiazhuang," he continued, "was built within thirty-four days after Tangshan disaster struck. The state covers all the expenses, from construction and education funds to students' monthly allowances. The school offers both primary and middle school courses in addition to a class for preschoolers.

"These orphans receive preferential treatment in job opportunities when they finish school. To date, fifteen hundred of them have been placed in jobs, and three hundred and fifty have become soldiers in the People's Liberation Army."

Matteo Ricci pecked at shadows on the window.

The Great Wall ascends from the Gulf of Bohai near Beidaihe and presents the first Pass Under Heaven. There, the barriers are overcast, stone backs round the mountains, wet children search behind the parapets for their families, massive memories shudder over the cleaves and breaks on the towers; the characters tucked on the inside mass hold culture and the last high promises from reach, and the water downwind is wicked at night.

The train station, classical portals, and pavilions near the beach are decorated with fresh flowers and evergreens. The ornamental posts and beams in the pavilions are covered with thick bright paint; enamel stalactites on the undersides of the corbels and rails.

The tourist houses, once the chinoiserie summer homes of the decadent colonists, were shaded under broad leaves, a short walk to the wide sand beach. The teachers located their rooms late that afternoon, washed and brushed for dinner, and then muttered over the cockroaches and cold water; earlier in the summer the count would have included cicadas, house lizards, and the mold dashed on the high walls.

Griever raised his chopsticks and poked the bloated side of a whole fish, golden fried on a cracked platter, but the head was dead, and the pectoral fins and opercula were sealed in a thick sweet sauce. The banquet room was cool; the rice, meat, vegetables, and fish dishes steamed the heads at the round table.

"Dead enough?" mocked Luther.

"Too dead," said the trickster. When he reached over the table for the shrimp and braised pork, the wide sleeve of his white shirt skimmed the carp and carrots.

"What did you expect?"

"Sashimi."

"Japs eat raw fish," snapped Gloome.

"Nevah, nevah," the trickster mocked.

"Griever is never earnest, never earnest," said Jack and Sugar Dee. "He never tells the truth, and even if he did no one would believe it."

"Truer words were never spoken," said the trickster with his hands raised, palms opened, in mock surrender. "Mao Zedong, that clever landlubber, rolled raw fish in rice to save the oil."

"Japs eat sushi," insisted Gloome.

"Hester, please describe the live carp cuisine, but first pass me that dish over there, the shredded pork, and the rice, and the garlic sauce."

"Mister Griever mean at very famous restaurants when fish comes to table," Hester explained over the steam, "fish mouth open and close and sides, the gills move, and sometimes this happens while people eat, maybe thirty minutes."

"What sort of fish is that?"

"Carp from lake."

"How does it move?"

"Secret," she said and then smiled. The teachers listened and watched perspiration gather at the scar on her cheek. "Fish head not fried, still alive."

"This must be a river carp," said the trickster as he prodded the dead head with a chopstick, "the heavy metal mutation for the tourists."

"Eating with you is like, is like," sputtered Sugar Dee, "is like going to the dump for lunch, or, or flushing a toilet in the middle of a meal."

"Would you like to hear about where the vegetables grow?" the trickster teased. "How about some wheat and

101

rice dried on the side of the asphalt roads, winnowed under the wheels of tourist buses."

"Never."

"How about the water?"

"Never mind."

"Salmonella ice cream on used sticks?"

"Listen, my mind is closed now for dinner."

"What a pity," whispered Luther, who took pleasure in discussions about pollution, sanitation, and diseases; he was obsessed with a dubious epidemic of hepatitis.

"Thieves cover their ears while stealing the bell," said the mind monkey, quoting from a proverb. "Close down your mind and pretend there is no sound in the sand."

"What does that mean?"

"Nevah mind," said Gingerie.

"Eat with your mouth closed," said Hannah, "there is enough poison and nonsense in the world, enough is enough at dinner." Two men waited at her side to see her breasts pitch and tumble when she leaned to the table. Their cheeks were red, necks erect like roosters.

Matteo Ricci was tied to a bed in the tourist house; the trickster remembered and bundled chitlins, miniature corn cakes, and sesame buns in his pockets. The table was stained in a wide circle, the carp was picked to the bone, the teachers mellowed and turned their table talk to historical revisions: the silk market, pinchbeck china, pirated books, and those marvelous traditions that died with the revolution; common mince, and bourgeois suspicions at the end of a lavish meal.

Matteo cocked his head and danced over the sesame buns on the bed; he pecked in clever measures, crunched the seeds, and then scratched the bleached bun aside in search of the chitlins. The trickster twisted a hair on his temple and rumors bucked with the shadows; crickets chirred in the moist seams beneath the windows. Overhead, cock-roaches churned the withered plaster. Wiverns roamed the wild corridors and healed old memories.

The bare warp snared the whole moon over heroic sil-houettes and patterns woven in the lace curtains; near the windows the trickster was pleated with a wise man in *clair de lune* laciniated pine boughs, and salt stains from a for-gotten storm. The cock landed crickets and then he pranced down to the sea behind the trickster, down to the bright stones, the small huddles on the sand.

"Matteo, he eats sand?" asked Hester.

"No, chitlins, buried chitlins."

"We do not have pets," she said and buried her bare feet in the cool sand. Hester covered her shins and tucked her dress under her thighs. The moon dashed over her cheeks and closed in her black hair.

"Chinese eat their pets."

"In America, you have many pets?"

"Even pet cemeteries," he said and pitched morsels in the air. The cock danced and landed the chitlins closer and closer to the water; on the last serve he soaked his feathers. "Headstones and cameos, mongrels with precious middle names, burial services, and real flowers, believe me."

Hester hitched her dress closer to her thighs and wrig-gled her toes under the sand. Matteo pecked at the wet fissures, his wattles shivered, membranes rended the water moons. She teased the cock and then waited in silence with her chin between her knees. Once more she moved her toes and the cock danced in wild circles, ticked his beak at their shadows on the sand.

"Hester."

"Mister Griever?"

"Remember that morning on the bus?" he asked and moved closer to the water. His shadow sliced the beach and

103

blocked the moon on her face. "Well, no one knew you, where to find you, and then like a dream, you appeared at the station this morning."

"Much business then," she said and uncovered her feet. She brushed the sand from her dress and then waded into the water to avoid his shadow. She had come to the beach to be alone, a rare favor as a student translator, but instead she humored his cock with her buried toes. He continued to reminisce their chance encounter while she waded deeper and watched her toes part, purled loose with the moon. She raised her dress higher and waded deeper until the wild moons lapped between her thighs and a cold undercurrent soused her groin. She trembled, rose higher on her toes, and then eased back to the current, deeper in the water, and urinated. Warm waves circled her thighs and the scent of onion and garlic washed to shore where the trickster roamed in a monologue, and his cock hunted in the shadows for crickets.

"Too much talk, right?"

"Not too much," she said and reached for her sandals. She dried her feet with a small towel and then wrung the scent of garlic water from the hem of her dress.

"Sometimes?"

"Sometimes, too much translation."

"Too much talk," he insisted.

"Not too much."

"Not too much?"

"Yes," she said and smiled.

"Hester."

"Mister Griever?"

"Please come to the pavilion with me," he pleaded and bowed with the cock on his shoulder. "The peach emperor created this place for the night."

Griever touched her hand and she trembled; he towed and she was stubborn in the sand. He smiled and walked backward with her to the Eagle Horn Pavilion. There, in the shadows of the broad leaves, back from the water, she warmed to his side; she leaned to his shoulder and marched one hand down his back.

"Sweet red blossoms," he said and pinched the moist petals. He smelled his fingers and then touched her nose. "What is the name of that one?"

"Red flowers."

"So late in the season."

"Red flowers."

"Too much translation," he said and moved to the entrance of the pavilion. The gate was closed and locked but the sides were open so he climbed over the wooden rail. Hester followed, and when she turned her buttocks on the rail he moved one hand over her thigh and palmed her groin. When her feet touched the wide plank floor he reached for her breasts with his other hand; he crouched between her knees, pushed her dress back, and nibbled on the inside of her thighs. The cock leaped from his shoulder and strutted on the rim of the pavilion.

Hester trembled on the wide rail, her breath raised blooms of moist ocean air. She loosened her hands, spread her thighs, opened wider. The muscles on her shoulders routed the memories of her father, and then her stomach shuddered, a silent and sensual endurance.

Griever lowered her panties and thrust his tongue into her wet vagina. She bounced on the rail and his nose brushed her clitoris; he burrowed and inhaled the wild humors. She danced on a broad amber beam with the peach emperor, a wild ichor burst from her sheath. He stood between her thighs and she touched his ripe testicles; his stout penis bounced on her wrist. The trickster beat her hard black nipples with his penis; lower, he pushed harder, once, twice, sperm burned the hollows, and then he hauled her down from the rail, bucked and bewailed the curtain.

105

"The wild moon," he whispered under her hair.

"Matteo Ricci strutted twice around the pavilion on a wide rail," he wrote later to China Browne. "He hopped down the stairs and hunted luminous crickets behind the lattice. So, this is one more colonial resort that took me in, but it was the wild heat of the whole moon and the smell of garlic last night near the sea that made this a real place."

PART 3

BAILU: WHITE DEW

Tientsin should be visited by night—the streets are all but blacked out, although here and there a lamp glows in the darkness—and the whole city, with its walled-up windows, its blind and leprous facades, seems to be a sleepwalker's dream. The paradox of this ghost city is that it is one of the major cities of the world, with more than three million inhabitants.

SIMON LEYS
Chinese Shadows

The death penalty is used extensively in the People's Republic of China. The laws provide for it to be imposed as a punishment for a number of political offences, as well as for ordinary criminal offences . . . people can now be executed for a wide range of offences, including theft, bribery, embezzlement, organizing a secret society, molesting women, gang fighting, drug trafficking, pimping or "passing on methods of committing crimes."

AMNESTY INTERNATIONAL
China: Violations of Human Rights

ℊ Victoria Park

Tianjin is partitioned in memories of lost relatives, colonial concessions, shadow capitalism, and painted faces from classical operas. Memories waver at night, never in the heart.

Griever considered the old street names on colonial maps, Marechal Foch, Saint Louis, Gaston Kahn, and then located the cathedral where the Lazarist Sisters of Saint Vincent de Paul had opened an orphanage.

John Hersey wrote that in their eagerness to win souls the sisters paid "a cash premium for each child brought in to them; and, what was worse, they were said to have paid to have sick and dying children carried to them, so they could baptize them *in articulo mortis*. In 1870, rumors were circulated that after conducting their mystic rites the nuns extracted the babies' eyes and hearts for purposes of witchery. Four men were arrested and beheaded. One man, under torture, confessed that he stole children and sold them to the verger of the cathedral."

"The city went wild," wrote Hersey, who was born in Tianjin, the child of missionaries. "The mob stripped the sisters naked, one by one, and in full sight of the surviving nuns ripped their bodies open, cut their breasts off, gouged their eyes out, and, finally, impaled them on long spears, hoisted them in the air, and threw them into the burning chapel of the orphanage."

Griever was astonished that the other missionaries survived that night; but he was even more surprised to find apple pie on the menu in the old colonial hotel restaurant. He folded the old map with care, pinched his ear, and ordered. The waitress returned with the last slice of pie. She stood at his side to practice her pronouns and verbs while he told stories from wild histories.

"Sian is beset with terra cotta warriors and inert tourists, cosmetic beasts in cold museums," the trickster muttered and searched for a wild hair on his temple, "but dreams never close down to serve the state."

"You eat pie."

"What kind of apples are these?"

"We eat pie."

"Not with chopsticks."

"You eat spoon."

"Confucius was a dream buried in wild histories," he said between enormous scoops of pie. "The old masters were buried with their eunuchs in fine fast dust. . . ."

"You like pie."

"Ceramic spears burst overhand."

"We like pie."

"Genealogies and reveries were cropped with each succession and revolution," he said and raised the spoon like a jade mace over the table.

"You mop up now."

"Where did you learn that?"

"You finish pie," she commanded. When she smiled, the mass of her cheeks rose close to her brows; she peered down at the white plate and tablecloth like an arctic hunter.

"Arenas, where millions of children are buried in unmarked graves, silent corners, streets and parks, have been renamed, but colonialism, that worm in the muscles of the

110

heart, persists in more than memories and printed words," he said and then cleaned the plate with his thumb.

Griever is a tattler in restaurants; when he eats alone he lectures to waitresses. Communism, trickeries, and comedies are his public themes; at the guest house, he argues with the teachers over capitalism.

"Communist soldiers," he roared in the baronial restaurant, "burned the common markers between racial and cultural concessions, wrenched the opium dealers, craven cloud chewers, and dismembered them on the road.

"Place names were purged," he bellowed to the vacant tables, "but nine colonial nations succeeded in their vaults and domes, spires, groins, cusps and lobes on arches, and in their moats and stunted trees, sculpturesque gardens, monolithic markets, the same old pillars hauled back from the shadows."

Victoria Park is the atrium in colonial concessions, carved from class reveries. The Astor House Hotel loomed there on London Meadows and Victoria Road, one block from the Hai He. The river bears the same name, which means "ocean river," but the roads have been renamed the Jianguo and Chengdu. The Astor House is now the Tianjin Hotel and Victoria Park has become a number. The hedgerows and imperial gardens, once sculpted with the same dedication as a hand tied carpet, were razed during the revolution. Colonial names were removed from directories, and common street maps became state secrets.

Hua Lian is the secular verger of Victoria Park, as the tourists remember the green, and warden of the bicycle parking lot at the corner. This is a comfortable position for an old blind woman who paints her face red and white, and who has refused to alter her memories from the concessions to please the new masters and shadow capitalists. The numbered factories, hotels, technologies, and conversions, were not visual; numbers, she told the cadres, are "blind, and repeated, not imagined."

Hua Lian, which means "picture" or "painted face," a traditional role for actors in classical operas, was born blind behind the park in a pleasant house where her mother was a servant to the president of the concession coal companies; her father served the green and the gardens and was a member of secret societies.

Zhou Enlai, Wu Chou, Hua Lian, and other celebrated actors, attended the Nankai Middle School in Tianjin. The principal, Zhang Boling, encouraged men and women to be activists. Zhou Enlai became premier of the People's Republic of China; Wu Chou, the warrior clown who studied shamanism and dharma trickeries, is the overseer of the campus gate; and Hua Lian is the verger of concession memories, trees, and the elephant slide, but, she insists, not the public toilets at Victoria Park.

Zhou Enlai invited Hua Lian to march in student protests. She was known as Hua Ci then, a nickname which means "painted word," because she was favored with a sixth sense, an acoustic kinesthesia; she could remember total conversations and visual details from several perspectives. Now, at her booth in the park, she pictures the past and recounts conversations. Zhou Enlai is there, or Feifei, as he was known when he wrote editorials for the student newspaper. He was arrested when he crawled under a gate at the governor's offices to demand the release of other activists. He was in prison isolation for six months, she remembers, and wrote messages on toilet paper. "In the beginning everyone gathered for a lecture given by Zhou Enlai on Marxism and historical materialism," she remembered his words.

"Tianjin has never been the same when he moved," she said, "but he wrote to me from other places. He told me he talked with Ernest Hemingway, and I could see the two of them together in Shanghai. Zhou with his new Sam Browne belt, and Hemingway with his wide moustache, but in the end, you know," she whispered, "Hemingway was no more than a word shadow. He was nervous and weakened with words, and we were cautious with word capitalists who attended revolutions. Hemingway wrote that the Communists 'always try to give the impression that they are the only ones who really fight.' Some writers raise the dust and wash their hands at the same time."

Hua Lian endured the revolutions behind a painted face. Her father was murdered and her mother died from fear. For months Hua Ci lived in Victoria Park with other lost children and ate bark from the trees.

She has never dressed for the reformation of place names, nor has she pretended to be a second in the public duels between the pragmatists and ideologists in each generation of power; her denial of the new number place names was at once overlooked because her blindness was seen as an inner exile, an eternal prison in a new land.

The bright blooms in the atrium, the dark walnut beams in the old hotel, warm pear pie, the cries of children on the bund, the sounds of horses on the old roads that circled the park, and other tastes and fancies, she has stationed in her visual memories. These lucid interior visions were not altered in word shadows or the revolution. Time bends in her marrow, a natural arch; the radiant gestures she remembers from causeries cannot be measured in the politics of names or the philosophies of written grammars.

Griever could not remember where he parked his bicycle. The Flying Pigeon was the same color as dozens of others in the even rows; the locks were even similar, bolted to the rear frame. Several saddles were covered with bright cloth and there were red pennons tied to some, but he had neglected to mark his bicycle for easier identification in the public lots.

113

Griever approached the old woman in the narrow booth at the entrance to the park. He leaned over the high counter and asked the warden, who held her head down, if she understood his common problem. The booth was dark, humid, and smelled of cosmetic paint and Springtime Thunder, a popular fragrance. He asked a second time, but did not wait for an answer because he remembered a wide crease on the chain guard of his bicycle. He inspected each green Flying Pigeon from one end of the lot to the other and found seven with similar creases. When he leaned down for a closer examination, the verger appeared at his side. She wore black cloth shoes, faded blue trousers, and a canvas chimere. There was a hole at the end of her right shoe from an uneven bound toe. Griever raised his head and there was the woman with the picture face, the peculiar woman who waited at the bus stop with a horsehair duster.

Hua Lian paints her face in the tradition of the classical opera for her duties in the park. She wears a bright red and white cosmetic mask to forbear public pities. When she laughs two dark molluscoid sockets open on her round face. The missionaries awarded her dark glass eyes when she graduated from middle school, but her father buried them in the park during the revolution to avoid criticism. She weeds the garden in search of her cosmetic eyes.

She learned the moves and positions of traditional operas; she painted the blind sockets dark blue and touched the loose skin at the rims with gold and silver glitter. Now, when she smiles and moves, the hollows reveal a personal constellation.

"The numbered factories," she said.

"Creases?"

"Bruises, marred and broken parts, come out the same," she chanted, "pragmatic designs from factory number two."

"Where did you learn that unusual accent," he queried

and then examined the blue sockets and the rich red paint on her cheeks, chin, and thin neck. Her brows were luminous, like a light beneath the water, and she wore one braid down her narrow back.

"The owners of those with the red standards have not paid the fee, you see," she explained with her head turned to one side like a clown. When she spoke she picked at a black wart near her collarbone.

"Where did you learn to speak English?"

"Do you own a bicycle?"

"Yes, somewhere, but I never knew about a fee," he said and moved closer. He held his breath and looked deep into the dark blue hollows on her face.

"Ten fen, please," she said and held out her hand.

"For a bicycle, no less," he complained and searched his pockets. "Here," he said and watched her hand move toward him; her smooth brown fingers seemed to sense the space and distance to his hand, like an insect, and then with a sudden pinch she had the note.

"Would you be staring at me?"

"Nothing more than close regard," he parried.

"What is your *meng mingzi?*"

"Listen," he said to avoid the words and questions he did not understand, "the colors, the lines, how can you see to paint such perfect pictures on your face?"

"Look," she responded, an eschewal of his tributes, "was it your pleasure to taste the pear pie at the Astor House Hotel?"

"Not pear, the last slice of apple pie."

"Pear pie, to be sure."

"Do you ever answer questions?"

"Confucius was asked that question once."

"What was his answer?"

"Words are rituals, catechisms a slow dance."

"Shit, who are you?"

115

"The other ritual," she said and moved toward the booth at the end of the row. She pulled the door closed behind her and leaned over the high counter.

"Wait," he pleaded, "what other ritual?"

"Blind rituals," she said.

"Where is my bicycle?" he asked, but she had lowered her head in silence. "Listen, tribal tricksters gossip from the heart, give me that much," he appealed over the counter. The words bounced back from an invisible cultural seal.

Griever found his bicycle in the third row under a red plastic standard. He pedaled a few blocks back toward the guest house but he could not continue because the visage of the blind woman appeared on windows, on buses, and at corners he passed. He circled the Small White House District, once the concession of the United States, and returned to the park. He sat on a wooden bench with a view of the booth and waited for the woman to emerge.

Griever counted thirteen immature blossoms planted in the hard circle behind the bench. Two stems were broken and the petals brushed the dust like tired soldiers. The trees were painted with lime, white trunks poised like ceremonial dancers. Broad leaves shadowed the back of a ceramic elephant in the center of the park. Breaks in the shadows unraveled on children, sprouted in wild red and blue, pink and green, from a metal chute that curved down from the mouth of the elephant.

The trickster leaned back on the bench and watched the elephant, and then he traced the massive shadows, classic revival columns, from the old concession coal companies on the corner. The Communist Party has occupied the building since the liberation; soldiers in oversized uniforms protected the oak portals. The shadows danced between machines, over chalk line caricatures on the cracked concrete, over cold histories at the end of a worn tether.

116

Griever held his breath until the train lurched through the mountain tunnel in a dream. In the darkness the seats turned to cages and the soldiers to monkeys. He was alone, supine on the last hard bench at the end of the coach. The animals stared and pointed. He moved to avoid their attention; when he looked out the window to find his place in the middle world, his face was captured in a simian reflection on the uneven pane. He frowned, smiled, winked, and the animal cast back the same expressions in reverse order.

Griever cocked his thumb like a pistol and aimed; the train pitched to the side on a curve, his trigger finger shot between the bars, and an old monkey severed it at the second knuckle with her stained teeth. He pulled his hand back; the train leaned in the opposite direction, and the finger rolled back from the cage. He recovered the stub and pinched it back in place with his other hand.

The monkeys howled and bounded in circles when an anile figure with pictures on her face entered at the end of the car, three times the distance of a common coach. The animals were becalmed when the old woman walked near their cages. She raised her right hand to her ear, a salute, and the monkeys folded their hands in silence. She moved to the end of the coach with her head down.

Griever waited with his hands folded near the window, and then when he recognized the red and white lines and blue sockets, the wart on her neck, he leaped from the bench to the aisle. He reached to touch her hand and noticed that his trigger finger was upside down; the nail was turned down and brushed her wrist.

"What is your *meng mingzi?*" she asked and raised her head. There were small lanterns at the bottom of the blue sockets on her face. The light wavered when she moved her head.

"What does that mean?" he asked.

"Your name, dream name," she answered and turned

117

back to the cages, "but it means more than that to the mind monkeys."

"More than what?" he asked and twisted his finger.

"What is your temper, show me your heart?"

"Listen," he responded, his standard salutation when he is troubled, "never mind my heart, my finger is on backward and nothing makes sense on this train."

Hua Lian touched the wart on her neck and the mind monkeys chattered while their cages turned back to seats. She moved down the aisle, stepped high over thresholds like an opera character, swished a horsehair duster in her hand, and when she passed their seats, the monkeys took the veil and became miniature nuns dressed in black habits and cowls with wide starched coifs shaped like speckled scallop shells.

"Jesus, Freud, Marx, and Mao," he said twice and counted the names with his fingers on the back of the seat, "this is a trick by the Gang of Four."

The train stopped at a crowded station. The nuns and other monkeys on the platform followed the old blind woman through the narrow streets of the town. Peasant women carried small lanterns and wailed behind the nuns. Children laughed at the monkeys under the veils.

Griever pushed through the crowd to be near the blind woman, but the closer he got the more animals he encountered. Then, when he reached to touch the braid with his turned finger, the nuns untied their cowls and stood naked; their bodies were covered with black hair.

"Yama, Yama, Yama, Yama," the monkeys chanted. Hundreds of them turned around him in a wide circle on the dirt road like a dark primal wheel.

Griever broke through the wheel and the dust shadows and ran to the end of the road. There, breathless in a small park, he clawed a panic hole between two fruit trees and

118

screamed into the earth. The leaves shivered overhead. At the bottom of the hole he found one glass eye.

Hua Lian touched him on the shoulders, and then she moved back to watch him awaken. He stretched like an animal, rolled over on his back, handed her the glass eye, and cradled his head in his hands.

"Confucius screamed underwater," declared Hua Lian. She stood behind the bench near the panic hole and polished the dark eye. She wore a red silk coat with the faces of monkeys embroidered on the collar and the sleeves.

"Goldfish ponds?" he asked through his hands.

"Rain barrels," she answered.

"You answered a question," he said and then remembered the monkeys on the train. He watched her hands and recounted several fast scenes from his dream; he could not picture when he cut the panic hole in the hard earth behind the bench.

"Your finger has turned."

"The nail was down," he said and pinched his finger. He could not understand how she knew about the events in his dream. There were no marks on his finger.

"Broken thoughts?" she asked with a wide smile. "You must be the one who freed the pears at the street market."

"Chickens, not pears," he responded.

"Free the pears and cocks, free words, free the shadows," she said. Her teeth chattered like a small treed animal.

Wide shadows reached over the park and shrouded the booth and the elephant slide. The breeze that moved the broad leaves increased the acrid smell of urine from the open toilet at the corner.

"Must have pissed on the train," he whispered and pictured the steam down the hole and remembered how he tried to count the crossbeams that passed under the coach;

119

more than a hundred ties before he closed and returned to his seat.

"Squeeze this under your nose," she said and handed him a small curved bundle of straw bound with a red ribbon.

"What is this?"

"*Da suan he ping*," she answered.

"What does that mean?"

"Garlic peace, for the toilet."

"No shit," he said and pinched the bundle. The scent raised his brows; his nostrils expanded with pleasure. He asked, but she would not reveal the herbal preparation.

Millions of fat flies swarmed over the dark mounds of human excrement in the toilet. The floor was wet with urine, several inches deep near the entrance. The servants who once cleaned the toilets are now the cadres; such menial duties were forbidden with liberation. The Gang of Four pressed doctors and teachers to serve socialism in public toilets, but since then the toilets have not been cleaned.

Griever held his breath and then pinched the garlic peace bundle under his nose to survive the stench; ammonia burned his eyes. He leaned back from the threshold and pissed hard and wide over the urine pond.

Hua Lian posed at the bus stop with a horsehair duster; exalted persons carried the duster, a token of refinement from the classical opera. She fingered the end and then swished the space around the double doors at the rear of each bus that stopped at the far corner of the park. Her manner was familiar to the regular passengers.

"Save this park," Griever said in a loud voice from behind. He pinched the garlic peace between sentences. "You said that last week when the bus stopped here, what did you mean?"

"Memories and trees."

"Why the trees?"

120

"Someone cuts parts from the trees at night."

"So, we can set a trap to catch the butchers," he suggested, "but why tell these strangers who pass on a bus?"

"Heart gossip," she said.

"Wait a minute," he insisted, "that's what I do, you got that line from me this afternoon."

"People will tell stories about that opera woman at the park and the person who cuts trees will hear and remember."

"Rather abstract conservation."

"Truth comes from peculiar places," she said as the next bus turned the corner near the park. "What I really do here is read faces on the bus."

"With one glass eye?"

"Watch me," she said and cut the space around his head with the horsehair duster, "like you watched those nuns on the train."

"Which reminds me," he said when he remembered a scene from the dark train, "in my dream this afternoon you had small blue lanterns in your eye sockets."

"Lantern is the word for eye in the cant of the old secret societies," she explained and then turned toward the street.

"Yama, what does the word mean?" he asked.

"Yama is the King of Darkness."

"Never mind," he said.

"The monkey nuns are on the bus," she said and cut small circles with the duster near the bus when it stopped.

"Where?"

"There, on the face of the driver."

"Never mind," he said.

"Who should we find on the next bus?"

"Confucius."

"The patient patriarch," she said and carved a figure from space with the horsehair duster, "the best voice for the rulers, the man of public altruism and filial pieties, the man who kissed stones but never broke them.''

"Do you see him?''

"Wait, he is not yet on this bus,'' she said. The diesel bus shuddered to a stop at the corner but she turned from the street and aimed the duster back toward the park. She turned the duster in small circles and followed a stout man who carried a small leather suitcase. His feet never seemed to leave the concrete as he hurried to meet the bus. He paused at the double doors, tilted his head to the side, smiled, and then he entered. The doors snapped closed on his shadow.

"Confucius he is not,'' exclaimed Griever.

"Watch him move,'' she said. Her duster seemed to hold the bus at the corner while she construed his paternal moves. "Notice how he bends his head to women and children, how he kowtows to power, to those in uniforms.''

"Kowtow indeed, how did you know that?''

"His heart gossip is bound in genealogies,'' she said and then lowered the duster. The engine started and the bus lurched from the curb. Hua Lian turned her head to the side and smiled; a child pressed her face to the window.

"Listen,'' he said, to avoid his insecurities, "let me see that duster, what's in that hair, some kind of radar?'' She handed him the duster; he waved it around his head and pictured Hester Hua Dan.

"Buddhist on the next bus.''

"Where?''

"The horsehair will find him,'' she said.

"What does a Buddhist look like?''

"Indifferent.''

"Never mind,'' he muttered and waved the duster in circles around his head. Two soldiers watched from the opposite corner.

"Watch for the man who is detached,'' she said, "the one

who has no interest in culture, women or children, the one who has a soul perched on his shoulder."

"How about those soldiers over there?"

"Communists are capitalists," she explained. "The soldiers serve the cadres, and the cadres down the line are the new shadow capitalists."

"Where are the Buddhists?"

"There," she said and pointed with her hand, "the man in the back with the uncombed hair and the basket of pears."

"Wait a minute," he moaned and lowered the duster, "that same man dropped his pears last week on the bus, and there are the old women who pushed me into a seat."

Griever moved closer but the double doors cracked closed; with the duster he conducted the bus as it pulled from the curb. The two old women remembered the trickster and covered their smiles. The woman with the puckered mouth was not wearing the black opal and blue stones.

♪ Opera Comique

Griever cleaved more observances than he inspired, but one practice continues to bear his name at the guest house. The Opera Comique de Hocus is held once or twice a week over dinner; the teachers read aloud their imagined and posted mail from lovers, celebrities, past presidents. The opera scenes with reels, cakewalks, crude tableaux, percussions, scored at each table, enlivens the cuisine and solemn winter months on campus.

Griever opened a stained envelope and read aloud a letter from his second cousin; the words were printed on a curve. Mouse Proof Martin, he explained, lived down river near Bad Medicine Lake on the White Earth Reservation. He was forced to attend a boarding school but never graduated. Smaller Whiteman, his father, marked the birth of his children on trees because he believed that people who were recorded in books lost their identities and bonds with the earth. Mother Whiteman, however, taught her children how to read from leaves; in the winter she wrote names, and the new words she copied from magazines, on leaves and scattered them on the hard snow near their cabin in the woods. The children collected the leaves and made stories from the words.

Mouse Proof Martin wrote that the "Chinese were here to see how the real skins lived on reservations, so we cooked some wild rice and pork for them, but no one, not even the translators, understood how rice could be wild. What can you tell people who think television is wild?"

Carnie tapped two plates with chopsticks and Luther beat the table with his hands. Gloome leaned back in his own verbal murk. Gingerie, who had been on a diet for several weeks, held a wide smile and wagged her pale head like a mannequin. Hannah danced around the tables and warbled the caesuras and several words from each letter. Egas Zhang and the stern cadres from the kitchen leaned closer to watch the pitch of her breasts when her blouse unfurled in a gauche pirouette.

"Here comes Mother Whiteman," said the trickster with a second letter from the reservation. "When you went over there you know what happened well they cut the juice at the electric can opener plant and the bingo hall that the tribe opened last year with our land claims money because they went broke and never paid the bill and we all got dumped out in the cold same as the old times and they closed down the can opener plant to keep the bingo going and the lake froze early and so we got unemployment now and Pink Babe got a new job selling shoes with no heels those new ones that are made that way and Miser Mae she washes new clothes in town to make them look worn down for sale and nothing else now. By By Mother Whiteman."

"Let her eat more white bread," Hannah warbled and turned one last time around the table. She buttoned her blouse and winked at the cadres from the kitchen.

Griever received a letter from China Browne, which he would not read aloud, and the two books he had ordered. One was *Monkey*, translated by Arthur Waley; and the other was the first volume of *The Journey to the West*, stories about a monk and a mind monkey, translated by Anthony D. Yu.

"China, would you believe that for a name?"

"China Browne, you told us about her little feet last week," Luther retorted, "and the week before that too, but tell me now, is this a new letter?"

"Eat yah tendons Luthah," said Gingerie.

"Griever, when will that rooster come to dinner roasted?" asked Gloome. He speared a tendon from a saucer. The tone of his voice was low, but the timbre seemed to loom from cracks in the earth and moved in the concrete and elbows at rest on the tables; so intense were some words that his voice vibrated in the utensils.

"Never."

"Rooster ragout."

"Never," repeated Griever, "Matteo Ricci is the best alarm you never had, but then, you seem to have as much trouble with chickens as you do with clocks."

Gloome has returned several alarm clocks to the store near the campus where he bought them. In spite of the tests at the store, he claimed that the alarms did not sound. Once or twice a week he ordered a driver to return the clock, and so she did, but with much embarrassment. The clerks in the store, however, circulated two clocks to appease the peculiar foreigner.

Gingerie, who revealed that she had earned a certificate in abnormal behavior, observed that when the old man returned the clocks, he expressed a real need for human attention. "Colin kills alarms to find friends, can we fault the man for that?"

Luther, who hated clocks and chickens, could not understand the need for an alarm when the music on the loudspeakers at dawn was enough to raise the dead. He was convinced that cocks caused diseases that antibiotics would never cure. "That cock is a curse to the health of the whole guest house."

Carnie announced that clocks were like prostitutes for the old man, one each night with no alarms. Gloome, his clock fetish, and the rooster, were the most recent accessions to the wild histories of the guest house.

Griever folded his letters, removed the stamps from the envelopes for the attendant at the guest house desk, and returned to his room to read the books he had received. He pushed the chair across the painted floor closer to the window, an escape distance in the cold concrete, and turned the first pages of *The Journey to the West*. He read about the origins of the earth and the birth of the mind monkey in the mountains while the cock wobbled and brushed the screen with his beak.

"There was on top of that very mountain an immortal stone, which measured thirty-six feet and five inches in height and twenty-four feet in circumference. . . . Since the creation of the world, it had been nourished for a long period by the seeds of Heaven and Earth and by the essences of the sun and the moon, until, quickened by divine inspiration, it became pregnant with a divine embryo. One day, it split open, giving birth to a stone egg about the size of a playing ball. Exposed to the wind, it was transformed into a stone monkey endowed with fully developed features and limbs. Having learned at once to climb and run, this monkey also bowed to the four quarters, while two beams of golden light flashed from his eyes to reach even the Palace of the Polestar. The light disturbed the Great Benevolent Sage of Heaven, the Celestial Jade Emperor of the Most Venerable Deva, who, attended by his divine ministers, was sitting in the Cloud Palace of the Golden Arches, in the Treasure Hall of the Divine Mists. . . .

"That monkey in the mountain was able to walk, run, and leap about: he fed on grass and shrubs, drank from the brooks and streams, gathered mountain flowers, and searched out fruits from trees. He made his companions the tiger and the lizard, the wolf and the leopard; he befriended the civet and the deer, and he called the gibbon and the baboon his kin. At night he slept beneath stony ridges, and in the morning he sauntered about the caves and the peaks. Truly, 'in the mountain there is no passing of time; the cold recedes, but one knows not the year.' "

Griever dreamed he was born from a stone on Flower Fruit Mountain. He became a mind monkey and chewed clouds and moved incredible distances between deep inhalations. One morning in his dream he became the master of monkeys; he talked backward, and he disturbed common manners in the world.

Mind monkey subdued dragons, tamed tigers, and started fires with little words in conversations with rulers and supplicants. In the middle of a discussion with Yama the King of Darkness the bed overturned and he escaped to a luminous tree in the mountains; there, close to his tribe, he heard the voice of death even in the flowers. He was driven to be immortal because nothing bored him more than the idea of an end; narrative conclusions were unnatural, he would never utter the last word, breathe the last breath, he would never pick flowers, the end was never his end.

Griever rolled over and over in the darkness of his dream and then tripped twice through the Hall of Divine Light on the uncertain course to the Jade Emperor in the Treasure Hall of Divine Mists. Warriors lowered more than a thousand cosmic nets, but no one captured the trickster that night.

Yama removed the name of the trickster from the Register of Death when he disrupted the Grand Festival of Immortal Peaches and stole the sacred fruit. Monkey became immortal when he ate the peaches; there were no ends in his stories.

Tripitaka, the monk who traveled with the mind monkey, named him the Pilgrim Sun when he became immortal. The mind monkey was pleased with his new name; he pretended to be a disciple and wandered with the monk in search of the sacred scriptures.

The Jade Emperor, however, was not pleased when he learned that the sacred peaches had been consumed without his permission. He called out his armies and the cosmic furies to capture the poacher, but it was an old woman, not the rulers, who tricked the immortal and wanton monkey to an end.

Bodhisattva Kuan Yin proposed to throw a sacred vase at him, but she learned that the mind monkey would break the vase with his imagination. Instead, she taught the monk the "true words for controlling the mind" of the monkey. The "tight fillet spell" would end the capricious adventures of the Pilgrim Sun trickster.

Griever dreamed that while he was the immortal mind monkey six robbers confronted the monk on a narrow mountain path. The robbers were small, mortal, with pinched cheeks and slow twisted smiles.

"Reckless hard-headed monk," said the first robber when he discovered that the monk and his monkey had nothing but dried fruit to steal.

"What is this?" asked the second robber.

"Needle entertainment?"

"Watch that monkey," said the fourth robber.

"Acupuncture man in disguise."

"Watch his feet," said the last robber.

"Watch me dance," said the Pilgrim Sun, and he touched his ear, twisted a strand of hair, and pulled out a small pin. He cut small figures around the robbers and the pin became a stout red iron rod. The monkey beat the six robbers to death in one breath.

"Kuan Yin is right," said the monk who did not approve of what the monkey had done. "You are a savage, undisciplined, and unwilling to be taught manners." Tripitaka rested near a tree and chewed on pieces of dried fruit. He chewed in silence and then he invited the monkey to share the fruit.

Pilgrim Sun opened the pouch and discovered beneath the dried fruit a silk coat and a luminous fillet inlaid with gold glitter. When he touched the headband, he could see blue bones and the blood flow in his fingers.

"Dear monk," said the mind monkey with his hand buried in the pouch, "let me put these on." His hands were luminous.

Tripitaka nodded his permission and continued to chew fruit. Then, when the monkey turned to pose in the coat with the fillet on his head, the monk recited the spell that he had learned from Kuan Yin. The fillet tightened with the recitation and the mind monkey screamed with pain.

Griever turned over in bed and was awakened from his dream; a band of pain around his head. He held his hands to his temples. When he was conscious and the pain escaped with the dream, he recounted the adventures of the mind monkey. The bats fluttered in wide circles and returned to their seams in the eaves of the guest house.

Matteo Ricci was perched on the balcony rail. He turned back to the window, extended his feathers with the dawn, and then crowed three times.

Griever turned the mattress, showered in cold water, and hurried down the stairs. He was ten minutes late for breakfast, but on weekends the kitchen workers were more tolerant because fewer teachers appeared for meals.

Gingerie and Gloome were seated at a corner table, their elbows tilted toward the margins and the remains of their conversation. Gingerie was on a starvation diet; she drank scented tea. Gloome was suspicious; he served his own meals from imported bottles and cans.

Griever moved a chair to their table and ordered one medium-boiled egg, toast, steamed bean buns, sweet noodle soup, and instant coffee with hot milk. He posted his own elbows on the table, leaned from side to side, and puckered his cheeks in a smile.

"Nevah serious are yah?" asked Gingerie.

"Nevah," he mocked.

"You never give up on the menu, do you?" said Gloome. His voice vibrated in the dark beneath the table. Two pale wattles wagged under his chin when he lighted a cigarette.

"Nevah," responded Griever.

"Every morning you order the same food," said Gloome, "but the eggs are always hard and cold like the rolls, the toast is burned, the soup tastes like soap water, and the instant coffee is the same everywhere, probably army surplus."

"They might make a mistake."

"Never," he boomed and brushed the table with the sides of his narrow hands. Cigarette smoke curled around his face and was absorbed in his thin hair.

"Your damned rooster woke me up again."

"Matteo Ricci sounds better than that horrible loud-speaker," said Griever. "Why is it that you never complain about that sunrise blast of patriotic music?"

"The loudspeaker is a human sound."

"Nevah," mocked Griever.

"Grievah is right," said Gingerie.

"Never."

"We shall see, and we shall see," Griever repeated while his breakfast was delivered to the table. The egg was hard and cold with a green yoke that dropped out and rolled across the table. The soup was lukewarm, and the toast had been rescued from the border of an acrid ornamental mold. He pushed the cracked plate aside, peeled the sweet coat from a bun, and nibbled at the dough down to the cold bean paste in the center.

℘ Sweet Piccolos

The teachers learned from the cadres at the guest house to conceal their uncertainties with cultural catch phrases: the moon cakes are marvelous; street crimes are uncommon here; the architecture is splendid; no narcotics in hotel lobbies; indeed, but no one could explain why there were so many locks on doors and drawers, and how a civilized nation could execute thousands for minor crimes.

The classrooms are locked at night, some doors even chained, others padlocked twice, three times, each with a separate key held by different cadres who must all be present to open the room. Some hotels lock the fire exits at night and stop the elevators; theaters lock the doors until the end of the opera. The teachers could not decide if they were prisoners, or if the rooms and buildings were locked for their protection.

The cadres bear the emblems of their new cultures—the devices and revised virtues of socialism, harmonious espaliers on loose brick barriers—with caution; the wise count locks and pockets to survive the political shell games. The mind monkeys, on the other hand, embroil the polished bric-a-brac and endure with pinched tokens.

Egas Zhang chews bear paws, one child, aphrodisiacs are promoted on state television, one child, women paint their nipples in the cities, one child, light bulbs and bicycles are

132

rationed, one child, students learn to swim to freedom in brackish water, one child, piglets are rented as contraceptives, one child, the trickster ordered an ultralight airplane.

Griever awakened from a dream, a chase scene in shallow water. He dressed in the dark and moved, like an animal at the treeline, down the carpeted stairs two hours before dawn. Hard insects marched on the cracked walls between the kitchen and the open toilets. He climbed through an open window; the doors were chained and locked from the outside.

The cool moist air was bitter with industrial chemicals. He cleared his throat several times, spat on the side of the guest house, and measured his steps past an open sewer to a narrow cobbled road that curved through several rows of small brick houses at the back of the pond. The moon was buried in mist and the few bare bulbs that illuminated the campus had been turned out at midnight. The road was uneven, bricks had been stolen. He was consumed in darkness, but he had practiced the night before when he carried a bamboo ladder from the construction site behind the new library to a broken window on the second floor of the administration building. There, at first light, he would control the loudspeakers on campus and substitute a march for the patriotic music that was broadcast at dawn around the nation. "One out of every five people in the world is awakened to 'The East is Red,'" the trickster wrote to China Browne, "but not this morning."

Griever climbed the ladder and opened the window. Inside, he used a flashlight to locate the amplifiers and patched a wire from his portable tape recorder to the sound system. He bolted the door, and then, too excited to resist the moment, he removed his clothes and danced nude from one end of the narrow room to the other. Breathless, he moved the chair closer to the amplifiers, held the cold flashlight under his arm, and counted to three before he threw the switches. He waited, double-checked the wires, but there was no sound; he tried the overhead light in the room, nothing. Then he remembered that electrical power to the administration building was out between midnight and one hour before dawn.

Griever leaned on the table below the window and waited for the power to be restored. He listened to the sounds of a steam engine in the distance. The night train drummed past the mountains and rolled down to the wild sea. He was there when the wheels of the coach touched the water and the windows shivered under pale waves of morning light. Cedar trees pitched on the wind and the landscape was transformed from ancient dust to a warm wet meadow.

China Browne was at the window.

Griever crossed the meadow and entered King's College Chapel at Cambridge from the Front Court. Inside, in the cool stone air, he counted cadence as he weaved between the tourists and rows of vacant chairs to the organ case screens. He extended his short arms and turned his shoulders in slow circles; with his head back, the roses carved on the wooden ceiling turned in the shadows.

China stood alone in front of the High Altar and the *Adoration of the Magi* by Rubens. The stained light from the high windows heaved on her thighs when she moved to the back row of the choir stalls.

"Touch this one," she whispered and then pointed to a carved statue, a dark wooden androgyne, at the end of the bench on the top row.

Griever mounted the stairs beneath the wooden cherubs and satyrs in the choir stall. There, at the corner, he pressed his moist hand to her thigh. The muscles on his shoulders and cheeks shivered like a horse down to water. The burnished thigh was warm, turned warmer in the high light. The androgyne rested on one knee, her head turned to the right shoulder. His hair was bound forward and

134

plaited loose with cloth; muscular arms pinched her breasts smaller at the post. One foot extended behind her buttocks; the enormous toes on the other foot, carved into the base of the stall, were broken and worn smooth.

Stained light carried the horizon.

Griever leaped from his dream when the recorder hissed. The tape crackled twice, and then, at high volume, the thirteen loudspeakers on campus sounded "The Stars and Stripes Forever" by John Philip Sousa, followed by "Semper Fidelis." The speakers shivered in the trees, boomed over the brackish pond, and the sound bounced out of time between buildings; the marches echoed through the windows of the dormitories. Rooms came to light in a blast of horns, windows opened on a paradiddle, and the sweet piccolo summoned men in uniforms.

Griever paraded around the room with a pencil raised like a baton until he heard the beat of feet and the sound of voices outside the door. He marked time to "Semper Fidelis" while the campus police searched for three keys to open the door. On the final beat of the drums, he disconnected the recorder, gathered his clothes and climbed down the ladder. He ran back to the construction site and then ducked from tree to tree. Several elders practiced their exercises on the rim of the pond, unaware that a nude mind monkey lurked in the shadows.

Griever climbed back through the window of the guest house and bounded the stairs. He could hear conversations in the rooms that he passed, and some laughter. The building was still dark, no one saw him leave or return to his apartment that morning.

Matteo Ricci stretched his neck and crowed four times when he heard the door close in the apartment. Griever turned on the lights with the first crow. Gloome roared his abhorrence on the second crow. Carnie mocked the cock and the roar on the third crow. On the fourth crow the trickster heard a hard knock at his door. He ran to the bathroom, threw cold water on his face, hair, and chest, and then he answered the door with a towel wrapped around his waist.

"Mister Griever," said Egas Zhang with a slight bow, "quite dark now, forgive me knock at door." He smiled, leaned back, and then lighted a cigarette.

"No more tapes," said Griever.

"No, no," he responded and blew smoke to the right side of the door, "music, you hear music this morning?"

"Yes, my compliments to the comrades in charge of the music, a real improvement over those *yi* and *er*, one and a two, national monotones by the Lawrence Welk of Tianjin." Griever loosened his towel and wiped his face and ears. He smiled behind the cloth.

"That music, you know that music?"

"Chinese Welk?"

"Not Chinese, but music you hear this morning."

"Sousa, sounded like Sousa to me."

"Soosha?"

"Listen, Zhang," said Griever in a firm tone of voice, "stop this cat and mouse, what is it you want with me?"

"Cat and mouse?"

"Soosha, you like music?" asked Griever.

"You have soosha?"

"Soosha is one of my favorites," the trickster said and buried his smile in the towel. "When you find that music, you remember to bring me some."

"Some person break into music room."

"No, not the music room," responded Griever.

"Some person walk on ladder."

"Walked on water?"

"No, bamboo ladder."

"Wait a minute, Zhang," he said with his head tilted to the side, "something is wrong here because you told me that we are safe here, you said there was never crime here, you said this was not like our country, but now you tell me that someone is breaking into rooms on the campus?"

"Yes, some person change music."

"Well, good for her," said Griever.

"Her, who is her?"

"Soosha is a woman, but never mind that now," he said with a smile and lowered his towel. "Forgive me, but I must return to my shower before all the hot water is gone."

"Mister Griever, excuse me."

"Soosha, find me some soosha," he said and closed the door. Griever stumbled to the bathroom with one hand on his mouth and the other on his stomach. He turned on the shower, flushed the toilet, and then burst into wild laughter.

ℊ Execution Caravan

Griever mounted a wooden camel and cocked a pose for a studio photograph, the last foreign teacher to complete his identification documents. He wigwagged his painted monkey face at the cautious children who moved underhand near the wild borders of the portrait landscapes. The studio, located on the second floor of a small department store near the restored concession cathedral, leaned to the nave, a crack from an earthquake. The desert bloomed on the aisle, and tropical animals roamed on the other border.

"No face paint, no, no," said the photographer through a studio translator. "Face paint, no no identification."

"No face paint, no picture picture."

"Mister Griever, children wait first pictures here," said the translator, a recent graduate from a language institute. Hester Hua Dan and Li Wen, who attend the institute, had told him stories about the trickster. His white shirt was too large, the collar folded under a wide plastic necktie. "Our photographer, he very busy man, must not waste time now."

Griever raised his arms like a simian and leaped over the wooden animals that grazed in various romantic and classical backgrounds. He brushed the painted curtains and moved a river; two panda bears and a dark pagoda wavered on a mountain.

The restless children pointed at the mind monkey and tried to mimic his movements; their laughter transformed the solemn studio. The parents, however, were embarrassed and held back their precious children from the rouse of the foreign devil who posed as a clown. The children bared their pink cheeks and lurched like leashed animals, better suited for the wild energies of a monkey in an opera than the colonial pose on the hard back of a white camel.

"Listen," Griever said to the translator, "tell our comrade photographer that the children would be disappointed to see my face without this monkey paint."

"Our photographer, he listens."

"Listen," he said and circled the children, "tell him that the parents will be very critical of him if their children see that their mind monkey is a foreign devil in disguise."

"Our photographer," responded the studio translator, "he said you are the mind monkey, he knows, now he understands."

"Understands what?"

"Face paint, yes, yes," said the translator.

"Smart man," said the trickster with a wide smile.

"Please, picture now," he said through the translator. The stout photographer was nervous, his gestures close to the waist. Sweat from his bare arms dripped down his fingers and marked the rough leather on his shoes.

The photographer moved his head like a tortoise; he smiled and directed the monkey to sit on a high stool in front of a huge box camera. The lights blazed and the shutter cracked louder than the release of a cocked hammer.

Griever posed with several children on the wooden animals and the miniature steam engine while he waited for the photograph to be developed and attached to his identification documents. The children smiled, their cheeks had been scrubbed to rose hues for the shadow catcher. The shutter cracked and captured their smiles.

Griever had started without breakfast because the gate-keeper promised to paint his face before the campus portal opened that morning. He locked his bicycle and combed his hair before he entered the gatehouse.

Wu Chou leaned over the brazier and started the char-coal to warm the water and face paint. The warrior clown wavered in blue smoke. He supped his tea, and then, with a bright red finger, he colored the cheeks, chin, forehead, and outsized nose of the trickster; he outlined with a narrow white and black band the broad contour of a heart on his face. Last, he painted a wide notch on his lower lip and formed a cardioid swell around his nostrils. The mixed-blood trickster became a mind monkey with a new mask, a tribal conversion in wild histories.

"Where is the mirror?" asked Griever.

"The Monkey King," said Wu Chou, "is never mute, he is white water, not a solemn pond, wild, he is wild, not a photograph."

"No mirrors?"

"No mirrors," said the warrior clown, "monkeys are immortal and immortals never appear in mirrors." He handed the mind monkey a beret, fashioned like a biretta with two blue tassels attached, and a lemon-colored raglan coat with blue piping on the collar and lapels. The coat was loose, the sleeves draped past his thumbs.

"Are monkeys silent?" asked Griever.

"Never."

"What language does a mind monkey speak?"

"Monkey never asks questions."

"Never?"

"Never, never," responded the warrior clown. "The

140

Monkey King has appetites, he devours the whole world, but he never lives on questions or silence."

"Mind monkey is a trickster."

"Mind monkey never satisfies the dreamers," the clown said, "he crosses roses with sparrows, and eats with his hands."

"Wait, wait, who is that in the horse cart?" Griever rushed to the door of the gatehouse and pointed with both hands at the figure in a shroud.

"Kangmei," said Wu Chou. He released the electronic lock and the woman on a miniature prairie schooner thrice whistled and the small horse pranced past the gatehouse.

"Kangmei, wait, wait," the trickster shouted but the horse pounded over the moat and disappeared in the traffic outside the campus. He turned and brushed an insect from the sleeve of his monkey coat; clouds of lemon dust swirled over the rough concrete threshold and settled in the dark corners.

"She is the first to leave at dawn."

"That woman was in a dream, she has a birchbark scroll from the bear cultures," the trickster whispered with one hand on his ear, "but she was never close enough to catch."

"She returns at dusk."

"Kangmei, what does that mean?"

"Resist the United States," bellowed the warrior clown.

"On a prairie schooner?"

"Kangmei was born at the end of the Korean War," he said over the brazier. "That was a time when we walked in the dark to avoid our enemies, and it was a time when some patriotic parents named their children to win the war."

"The war ended, so why the shroud?"

"She hides her face," whispered Wu Chou.

"Why?"

"Because, she has blond hair." He supped the last black

141

tea from the bowl, lighted a cigarette, and smiled in the blue smoke.

"Blond Chinese?"

"Her father was an American."

"Some resistance."

"He was stateless, one of the few foreign devils here during the war," added the warrior clown and then he opened the gate for a government official in a black limousine. "More than that would be a state secret."

Battle Wilson, Oklahoma-born Sinophile, poet, idealist, and petroleum engineer, opposed the Korean War and near the end became a stateless victim of socialist justice. His stories open with an inheritance of Manchu Dynasty Silver Dollars and close in an earthquake at Tangshan.

Battle, the plains dreamer with a tribal nickname, was awakened by Mao Zedong and the idealism of the revolution; so, he smuggled his legacy to London. There, in search of cultural emblems, he prowled in the dark corridors of the British Museum and learned about the manuscripts that Sir Aurel Stein had stolen from the Kingdom of Khotan, and other cities on the silk roads in Chinese Turkestan. Battle had never stolen before, so it was a bold move when he seized one birchbark scroll, several terra cotta bear figures, and a black opal ring circled with lapis lazuli stones from the museum cases, and deposited his Manchu Dynasty Dollars, struck with the seal of the Imperial Dragon. Two weeks later he was in the land of his wild and exotic fancies with the opal on his finger and the scroll in a holster at his side.

Battle posed as a writer and advanced his romantic poems and stories about the treasures he had liberated when he was held by soldiers at the frontier border.

"Look at these stones," he said and removed his leather mittens. The museum identification label was attached to the band. The black opal blazed; the soldiers turned to the side, avoided the light, and reported to their superiors, and others in command, higher and higher in the revolution, until the adventurer reached a secure and imaginative listener.

Battle said that Ding Ling, the feminist writer and winner of the Stalin Prize for her novel *Sun Over the Sangkan River*, heard the stories and invited him to tell more. He read a few poems, and in turn, she reported the information to the high cadres who reviewed writers and their stories.

Battle bowed with his head to the side when he met Mao Zedong in the Great Hall of the People at Tiananmen Square, but no one seemed to notice because he was so much taller than the peasant leader. "Chairman Mao," he said to the translator, "we are one with the earth, count me in on the revolution."

"Chairman Mao," the translator responded, "does not trust romantic intellectuals, he does not believe in universal human emotions, but he would appreciate information about petroleum exploration."

"He would?"

"Yes."

"When did he say that?"

"You are a petroleum engineer?"

"Yes, a poet and drill bit specialist."

"Indeed," said the translator, and within hours the foreigner was on a truck to the new oil fields in Yumen and the Qaidamu Basin. There, he lived in a mud hut, inhaled fine salt dust from the desert, and drilled oil for the revolution.

Battle labored with romantic pride; he waited to be honored, but he was never even trusted. Later, stateless and discontented, he was relocated in Tianjin and ordered to build petrochemical plants. There, on a lonesome night

143

near the river, he met the wife of Egas Zhang. Yan lived alone with her daughter then; Egas was a translator at a railroad construction site in Africa.

Battle visited his lover late at night under the trees in Victoria Park; on their first night together she became pregnant. Yan refused an abortion; she endured the humiliation, a broken reed in the revolution, and gave birth to a daughter in the public hospital.

Egas returned two years later. He hated the blond child, but he took some pleasure in the social scandal; he could abuse his wife and children with impunity. "Kangmei, Kangmei, the mixedblood barbarian," he railed.

Battle, meanwhile, was banished to a labor reform camp in Tangshan. Seven times, with the help of Hua Lian, he visited his daughter in Victoria Park. There, on his last visit, he gave her his precious poems, and the birchbark scroll he had removed from the British Museum. The black opal and the terra cotta bears he gave to a translator in the Great Hall of the People. No one believed his stories about the bears and stone cultures on the wild silk roads. Battle died in the earthquake and was buried in an unmarked grave with several thousand other victims.

From the car, a child peered through the curtains with her chin perched on the rear window channel. She shivered with nervous laughter when she saw the monkey at the threshold of the gatehouse. The chauffeur, trained to respond to old whims and new socialist spoils, stopped the limousine. He opened the rear door and the child bounced out to capture the clown. She clapped her thick red hands and hopped around the monkey. The scarlet ribbon on the back of her head broke loose and currents of dense hair concealed her wet chin. When the dance circle closed, the child had bound the monkey at the knees with rope; she shivered and pounded her head on his rump and thighs to move him from the gatehouse. The uniformed chauffeur pretended to scold the child; when she punched the monkey twice in the groin, he hauled her back to the limousine, tied her hair back, closed the curtains, and locked the rear doors.

Griever snickered when he examined the monkey photograph on his new identification card. He pushed his holster back, brushed his sleeves, unlocked his bicycle, mounted one pedal and was prepared to leave when three children from the studio seized the fenders and wheels. Their hot hands roamed over the metal, from the cold handlebar to his sleeves, closer to his painted face. One child, the shortest of the three, moved back a few paces and then rushed at the monkey and knocked him down. The children tittered and wriggled over the monkey and his machine like a litter of rodents.

Griever laughed, and the louder he roared the more he lost his strength to hold back the children. Hundreds of people heard his wild voice and gathered in a wide circle to watch the supine scene on the concrete. Two children held his arms down while the runt sat on his stomach and with his blunt fingers reached to touch his face and pinch his nose.

"Sun Wukong," the audience chanted.

"Mister Monkey King," called the translator from the studio as he pushed through the crowd, "what happens to bicycle?"

"The children wanted more than pictures," responded the mind monkey from the concrete. He pitched his stomach, raised his arms, and the three children rolled over and vanished in the blue mass.

The translator raised the bicycle and brushed the fenders with his white gloves. The audience separated but then returned in a few minutes when a policeman entered the

145

circle. He asked the translator to explain what had happened and then he demanded identification.

"You show card now," said the translator.

"Not a chance," responded Griever.

"Must show card." The translator presented his card to the policeman who removed his white gloves to examine the photograph, red chops and seals.

Griever mounted one pedal on his bicycle to move when the policeman seized the handlebar; the crowd moved closer. The man was nervous; he held on with both hands. The front wheel was parked in his crotch.

"Show bicycle card," chattered the translator.

"Bicycle card?"

"Mister Griever, policeman take bicycle with no card."

"Who is this asshole?"

"Public Security Bureau," explained the translator who was relieved that the policeman had turned his attention to the foreigner. "Very strong, you must answer questions."

Two more uniformed policemen from the Tianjin Public Security Bureau broke through the circle and surrounded the foreign mind monkey on his bicycle. While the first policeman explained to the other policeman what had happened, the worried translator moved backward and disappeared in the crowd.

"Never heard about a bicycle card," said the monkey several times but no one translated his last minute pleas. "Listen, there is no need for this trouble, would you and your wife like free tickets to the movies?"

Griever dismounted and presented his new identification card to the policeman with the most pockets, who opened the red plastic wallet to examine the photograph and chops. He passed the wallet to the other policemen, and then flashed the photograph of the monkey to the audience. The policemen and the audience broke into loud laughter.

"Sun Wukong," the audience chanted. The three policemen saluted the mind monkey and returned his identification wallet, but his bicycle was impounded until he obtained a proper license from the Public Security Bureau. The monkey leaned back on his heels and returned the salutes with both hands. He moved outside the circle, pinched and folded one ear, and then searched for a wild strand of hair on his right temple.

Griever pillowed the golden curtains at the corner near the French Cathedral, and tied the loose colonial seams at the end of Marechal Foch. Three pretenders to the old cathedral see trailed the Monkey King down Gaston Kahn, which, two blocks behind him, became Elgin Road on the other side of Saint Louis Boulevard. He wandered beneath the hallowed cantilevers of the new aristocracies, the mansard moles. The scent of rue and *bouquets garnis* embalmed the end of each intersection. Two sweepers in white masks came to his side when he unfolded the old concessions map; the monkey marked the last concession chancel.

The Monkey King and his five disciples turned right on old Matsushima and canted a haiku poem on the road that bound the silent river to the locked campus.

Griever smelled sweet ginger, aromatic oils, and clean water down the four blocks to the wide curve in the river which divided the Japanese and Italian concessions. A boat with luminous oars and hundreds of sampan, with children at the prows, women *midchuan*, and men at the sterns, moved like water striders. Narrow covers were moored on the bund, a homeland between the concessions.

The mind monkey twisted a wild hair on his temple and turned right on Chaylard in the French concession, crossed Julliet and Verdun, starched muslin and pleated lace, and pranced high like a *boulevardier* to Saint Louis, which became Bristol in the British concession. There, at the curb, two angular women in loose print dresses pursued the monkey, the three pretenders to the see, and the two sweepers. One block below Davenport on Recreation Road, the Monkey King encountered a grim parade at the intersection of Oxford and Cambridge.

Six military trucks, three black limousines, and dozens of other government vehicles assembled at the train station and moved in a column over Liberation Bridge at Jiefang Road, which was Bourgeois Boulevard in one concession and Victoria Road in the other, and toured the financial district. Thousands of people were crowded on the embankment, on both sides of the roads, and hundreds of administrators, dressed in white shirts and black ties, leaned from windows to watch the execution caravan.

There were eight prisoners on each open truck, four on each side, and eight uniformed soldiers. The prisoners were bound from behind with a rope attached to their necks. Most of them looked down at the new boots on the guards; the few who dared to search for a smile on the road, were pushed to their knees. These prisoners, and hundreds more in other cities, had been sentenced to death for various crimes. The prosecution rallies, trials, public sentences, and execution parades were scheduled at the same time around the country.

The execution caravan turned right at Chengdu Road at Victoria Park on London Meadows in the old concession and moved at reduced speed past the local headquarters of the Chinese Communist Party. Companies of soldiers stood erect in front of the concession columns, their weapons raised to menace the prisoners, but the review was broken when the witnesses choked on the diesel exhaust from the trucks.

The caravan continued down London Meadows for two blocks and then turned left to a museum at the corner of Elgin and Oxford. There, the prisoners were butted from the trucks and herded to the center of an outdoor amphitheater. When their names and crimes were announced, and their sentences were pronounced over the loud-speakers, the audience applauded and cheered.

Millions of citizens heard the sentences broadcast over radio and television. Cheers broke clean from apartment windows, wild applause tripped from high balconies, and old voices echoed low between the narrow brick houses like the sound of water down the grates. Death loomed on the concession roads and crossed into the middle world with a horrible sneer.

The mind monkey and his disciples heard the applause on the road two blocks from the amphitheater. Six policemen dressed in starched white coats blocked the intersection. The two sweepers were told that the execution caravan would continue down Oxford to Cambridge, where the monkey waited, and then turn at Race Course Road to the United Kingdom Cemetery, a hallowed concession hidden behind high brick walls near the horse barns, where the accused were to be executed before dark.

The two sweepers handed the mind monkey a patch of paper and then scattered other copies in the crowded intersection. The monkey unfolded the thin patch, as sheer as toilet paper, and read a statement on capital punishment written by a foreign journalist who worked for Xinhua, the government news service. The statement had been posted on bulletin boards in several cities.

The Monkey King bounced his head backward and twisted three strands of hair on his temple. His chin seemed to crack with heat, and when he moved in the crowd, he turned like a coil closer to the corner and the caravan route. The policemen were amused with the foreign devil in the monkey face when he read the news out loud behind the barriers, but their brows shivered when several voices called out the translation to the crowd.

"I could cry," the monkey read from the thin patch of

paper. "I heard the day before yesterday that there were
hundreds of arrests in Beijing. Yesterday, I heard there
were thirty people executed. . . . You tried thirty young
men in the stadium in San Li Tun in front of fifty-thousand
people. How could thirty people get a fair trial in one day?

"I would sooner be dead than submit to tyranny. A legal
system that can try thirty people in half a day, and commit
them all to their graves as a result of that trial, is a tyran-
nical system. . . .

"Do your police never make a mistake? Are your police
filled with virtue and do they have all the wisdom of
Confucius?

"A friend said to me that it is unfortunate that before
you had your socialist revolution you didn't have the op-
portunity of knowing a period of being bourgeois and have
the chance of picking up some bourgeois values, like freedom of speech, freedom of the press, civil liberties and an
abhorrence of capital punishment."

The sun broke on the thin paper and the words dissolved
at the intersection. Several policemen moved to detain the
monkey, but the sound of diesel engines and the approach
of the execution caravan distracted them from their mission. Even so, the three pretenders pulled the monkey back
from the front of the crowd, back from the barriers.

The Monkey King was perched on a ceramic trash container when the six open trucks approached the intersection. He saluted the officers in the limousines at the head of
the caravan, and then he leaped from the container, over
the people seated at the curb, and danced in the street like a
warrior clown. He turned his head so fast the sides of his
smile connected at the back of his head. The fronts and
sides of the trucks were covered with execution broadsides,
photographs, and short criminal biographies of the accused,
with wide red ticks on their faces, the marks of death.

The mind monkey danced around the first truck three

times, but on the fourth turn he climbed over the side and balanced on one foot on top of the cab. The monkey mimicked the soldiers; when the soldiers waved their rifles, he waved back. When an officer ordered him down, the monkey pranced in place and demanded the release of the prisoners.

"The Jade Emperor and Sun Wukong in the Treasure Hall of Divine Mists order you to release these prisoners," said the Monkey King. The two sweepers called out their translations from both sides of the road. Some citizens covered their mouths and snickered, and a few soldiers smiled, but the officers with the most pockets had the most to lose and stopped the execution caravan to remove the monkey.

The soldiers could not reach the monkey, but when the truck lurched forward he lost his balance and tumbled back in the bed of the truck. The prisoners applauded with their knees. The soldiers seized the monkey and marched him to the side of the road where he was interrogated.

"Your name, the officer would like to know your name," said one pretender who had agreed to serve as a translator. The officer with the most pockets pressed his thumbs on the monkey to examine the paint.

"White Earth Monkey King," said Griever.

"The officer is not amused, you would be wise to tell him your name and show him your identification card," the pretender insisted, but he winked at the monkey, certain that there were others in the crowd who would understand the tone of his translations. The caravan was blocked at the corner because hundreds of citizens had gathered around the monkey and the soldiers.

"Wei Jingsheng," said the monkey.

"Please explain?" asked the translator.

"Well, we were electricians and editors of the new magazine *Exploration* when we were arrested five years ago," said the monkey to the citizens in the circle. He smiled and gestured to those who stood behind the soldiers. "We opposed socialism and the leaders of the Chinese Communist Party, and we argued for five modernizations, one more than economic rights, we wanted the rights of democracies, and so we were arrested. . . ."

"No, no, the face paint, explain the paint."

"Sun Wukong," said the monkey. He stood on one foot and saluted the officer. The truck engines rattled and diesel smoke escaped over the broken circle of soldiers.

"An American Monkey King?"

"Sir, please forgive me, my real name is Fu Yuehua," said the monkey with his head down. "Five years ago we organized a peasant demonstration to end hunger and persecution, we demanded human rights but instead we were sentenced to a labor camp."

Griever presented his identification card to the officer and leaned back on his heels with his hands over his ears. The mind monkey had pushed reason over the rim, but now he uncocked his head and turned complaisant. The officer repressed a smile when he saw the photograph inside the red wallet; the soldiers, and several cautious citizens leaned closer to see the picture.

Two disciples, one angular woman in a print dress, and the second pretender to the see, tittered, a docile sound, like wind driven newspaper under a park bench. Their manner spread to the others in the circle. The prisoners traded wild smiles, and soon the soldiers, and the press at the intersection, were doubled over in laughter. The mind monkey clicked his teeth, recovered his identification card, and mounted the ceramic trash container once more. The trucks roared and the soldiers broke the circle to continue the execution caravan.

The Monkey King leaped to the street a second time and mounted the hood of the third truck. "Confucius and Mao

Zedong were liars," he shouted, "no one here will ever be free." The driver honked the horn, and the soldiers cocked their rifles; the monkey was braced like a hood ornament, but when the caravan turned down Race Course Road he wheeled to the side, opened the door, and pulled the startled driver from the truck. The soldiers in the back of the truck were pitched over the side when the truck turned twice at high speed, swerved to the right, and then circled back through the concessions. Hundreds of citizens chased the monkey truck and blocked the soldiers and other vehicles. The pursuers were lost when the truck turned near the river and roared down Woodrow Wilson Drive.

The Monkey whistled a march and bounced on the hard seat as the truck rumbled through a construction site and shuddered to a stop inches from a brick wall of an abandoned warehouse, the remains of the godowns from the concessions.

The prisoners on the truck, seven men and one woman, were silent while the monkey untied their swollen hands. Freed, the three rapists escaped on a small river boat, the heroin dealer brushed his hair and wandered down the bund, the one murderer walked back to the main road, but the prostitute, the robber, and an art historian who exported stolen cultural relics remained on the back of the truck with the mind monkey.

The prostitute was dressed in loose trousers, a black shirt, and cloth shoes. She opened her thighs and patted the sides of her head where the soldiers had shorn her hair with a scissors.

"I survived the revolution as a translator," she said in a hoarse whisper to the monkey. "Then came the new capitalists and we organized the Homework Service Company, we hired peasant women to work as domestics, nannies, and maids."

"Nannies for the cadres?"

153

"The nannies were accused of prostitution when the three men who hired them were exposed as corrupt managers of government factories, the soldiers arrested me as the organizer. From our arrest to a death sentence took less than a week."

"But now you are free," said the monkey.

"No one is free."

"You are still alive to trick the world."

"Who are you?" asked the prostitute.

"Lord Piltdown, at your service."

"Really?"

"Sun Wukong, that is my real name."

"Monkey Kings are myths for the poor and oppressed," said the prostitute. She pinched the loose skin on her bare forearms and laid her head back on the side rail of the truck to catch her breath; and with each short breath she remembered the missionaries who saved her when she was a child abandoned on the frozen streets. Even now, borne on the execution truck between memories and the last curtain, and the moment the death sentence was pronounced at the public trial, she worried that she would lose her breath and break down. The monkey touched her shoulder; she turned her head and shivered.

"Mind monkeys are immortal," he mocked.

"Marvelous death," she whispered.

The robber was isolated, a detached watch at the dark and distant end of the truck. His bare toes were spread wide on the metal bed. He twisted his fingers, and then pulled each of them until the knuckles cracked. The sound rattled on the cool bricks in the warehouse.

"Where have we met?" the monkey asked the robber.

"He never speaks," said the art historian. "He has not said one word since he was sentenced this morning in the amphitheater, his voice must have died first."

"What was the crime?"

154

"He stole an opal ring from an old woman."

"The black opal?"

"That, he sold to me."

"He carried a golden water bottle," the monkey reminisced at the back of the truck, "and he dropped green pears on the bus, but how could he steal the opal?"

"He told the old woman he loved her," he said with a thin smile and hobbled in small circles at the end of the truck, "and moved into her apartment to be closer to the ring and other valuables."

"Death for a black opal?"

"High-priced indeed, but she was the seventh old woman he so loved in the past few months," the historian explained and then asked the monkey for a cigarette.

The art historian halted at the end of the truck when he heard voices in the distance. He was leaden, a tractable animal on the trail; then, when he heard the rapid crack of rifle fire, he rushed back to his seat and waited there with his hands folded. The mind monkey leaped from the side of the truck and watched the hunched soldiers move down the bund closer to the three rapists who had fallen from the boat into the thick water. The rapists swam toward shore; the soldiers carried out the death sentence at the site. Hundreds of bullets hit the rapists, their heads burst, brains steamed, blood stained the river.

The Monkey King soared through an open window at the end of the warehouse and moved over the rims and margins in his memories, but when he tried to hold back his shadow, the low sun carried his pitch over the corners; his arms folded at the entrance to the Friendship Store, an exclusive market for foreigners, and broke at the curb. He ducked into a bicycle shop to avoid three teachers, and then he turned the corner and hurried to Victoria Park on the other side of the street.

"The soldiers come to search," said Hua Lian and pulled

155

the monkey into the narrow booth at the entrance to the park.

"Where?"

"The toilets," she said and pushed him down beneath her feet to the rough concrete. She leaned on the counter and waited.

"Shit, who would hide there?"

"Now the elephant slide," she whispered.

"Bastards," he said, but sealed his mouth when she kicked him once and rested her foot on his neck. The odor of her feet brewed with the smell of paint in the booth. When he heard the soldiers approach, he coiled like an insect under her apron and wide red silk coat with the faces of monkeys embroidered on the collar and sleeves. His nose swelled from the smell of her crotch, racier than her hard feet. He found two cans in the corner and dusted her feet with Double Happiness Pearl Foot Powder and her crotch with Springtime Thunder.

When the soldiers hammered on the counter with their weapons, she leaned closer to their faces and smiled. No, she had not seen a man with a monkey face, but when she did, she told the soldiers, she would capture him, hold him down, and have sex with him until he turned human. The soldiers laughed and she continued her stories. She told them that a monkey would never come near her because blind women have too much sexual power. The soldiers laughed once more and moved back from the booth, back from her breath and luminous brows.

Hua Lian waited on the corner for Kangmei to circle the park. She arrived at dusk, as usual, and the two whispered twice around the park before the monkey was invited to ride back to the campus in the prairie schooner.

"You must not talk," said Hua Lian.

"No talk?"

156

"Must ride back in silence."

"Silence, then," he said and climbed into the back of the wagon. He waved from the shadows behind the curtain. He was fast asleep when the prairie schooner passed through the campus gate and stopped beneath the trees near the guest house.

Griever climbed down and watched the prairie schooner round the pond and disappear. He routed two shallow holes near the trees and roared into each one. His voice shivered with pain and resounded on the black water and echoed back past the gatehouse to the concessions and the river.

Silence seized the moist air under the bare broken light bulb at the end of the road. The mind monkey pinched his hands under his arms and slipped through the dark to the side entrance of the guest house.

Matteo Ricci crowed when he entered the apartment. The rooster followed him to the bathroom and perched on the rim of the sink. He pecked at images in the high mirror. The white and black paint had melted into the red, and the notch was smeared on his chin. He scrubbed the fingerprints on his cheeks, the prints from the officer, and flushed the evidence down the drain.

PART 4

QIUFEN: AUTUMN EQUINOX

The Peking branch of Maxim's is a replica
of the famous Parisian restaurant now
owned by fashion designer Pierre
Cardin. . . . "If I can put a Maxim's in
Peking, I can put a Maxim's on the moon,"
he boasted to his guests at the inaugural
banquet. "Close your eyes and you are in
Paris. It is Paris right down to the smallest
detail. . . . China is changing. My idea
would have been unthinkable a few years
ago. In ten years this country will be like
Japan."

ORVILLE SCHELL
To Get Rich Is Glorious

Each cell kept a little box for toenail
parings, passed around from man to man as
he snipped himself. At the end of every
month the warder collected the boxes and
turned them over to the central prison
authority for sale to the outside. Mixed
with other equally exotic ingredients, the
toenails were used in traditional Chinese
medicine. I never did know what they were
supposed to cure, but it was enough that
they paid us a movie every four months—a
dreary propaganda movie, to be sure . . .
but it was still a break from the routine.

BAO RUO-WANG, JEAN
PASQUALINI
Prisoner of Mao

◖ Obo Island

Shuishang Water Park bears a horde of tourists, seven wild animals, three birds in a mesh, and dead water; tired pandas thumb the stone walls, tigers wheeze over the children at the posterns, sullen eagles hack the narrow bamboo beams with their wicked beaks, and keels dissolve on the dark blue shores.

Griever rowed a rented plastic boat close to shore in the thick water. The oars screeched in the rusted locks; he drifted in silence under an arched wooden bridge. Overhead, tourists paused on the rail to chatter, hand over hand, and watch the cock high in the bow of the boat. The boards rattled when the tourists crossed over. On the underside, rats roamed in the shadows with bits of steamed *mantou* and other morsels to their colonies on the islet bandstand.

"Mao lives," the trickster announced to the tourists and the rats as he passed under. He raised an oar to tease the slower rodents on the curved support beams.

"*Lao shu, lao shu,* 'rats, rats,'" a man warned from behind the trees on the other end of the bridge. He crouched with a rifle, aimed, and fired three times.

Sandie, a name he had earned from a comic opera, the most sincere character in the stories about the mind monkey, was a government rat hunter. When he raised his rifle, the trickster ducked his head, lost his balance on the

161

second shot, and tumbled into the shallow water. At the same time, two dead rats dropped from the beam; one bounced on the boat near the rooster.

"Asshole, you missed one," shouted the trickster as he sloshed close to shore. Blood splashed when the second rat hit the water.

"*Zhua zhu lao shu*," said the hunter. He shouldered his rifle and waded into the water to hold the boat and retrieve the rats he had shot.

Matteo Ricci, perched on the bow with his wings drawn, pecked at the rodent and the hunter. The cock shivered, raised his beak, and danced down the bloodied plastic gunwales.

"English, asshole," the trickster complained.

"Catch the rats, asshole," the hunter translated with a wild uneven smile. His neck and arms were thick, but his shins were lank, tapered like blades, and his feet were too narrow to walk in water.

"Mao lives," repeated the trickster and raised one rat from the water. Shattered bone and brain marbled the blue mud on shore. "No head here to mount."

"Sorry about that," said the hunter, "no harm intended." He hauled the boat to shore; overhead, the tourists applauded the wild hunter.

"Too much for two rodents."

"Rats are worth more than chickens."

"Dead or alive?"

"Rat steaks and hides," said the hunter.

"Steaks?"

"Dim sum at the guest house."

"Never."

"Rat stroganoff at Maxim's de Beijing."

"Now that sounds right."

"Designer shoes, no less."

"No less," mocked the trickster.

162

"Berkeley."

"What about Berkeley?"

"You were about to ask me," said the hunter, "where in the world did you learn how to speak with such ease, and the answer is simple. . . ."

"University of California."

"Political science and economics," said the hunter, eager to please an audience, "but these are peculiar times."

"No shit?"

"No shit about the rat steaks and the shoes either," he said, "but listen, your clothes are wet, so come with me now."

"Where?"

"Obo Island on the other side of the water park," he said and pointed with his blunt forehead. He stacked the rats in the bow with thirteen others from an earlier hunt and pushed the plastic boat back into the thick dark water.

"Wait, this is a rented boat."

"Mister Griever," he responded, "never mind now, you are with a government rat hunter and the rent on the boat is of no concern."

"How did you know my name?"

Sandie moved an ovine smile from one side of his face to the other as he rowed; the oars screeched in the locks. The trickster was silent, perched at the stern in wet clothes; his shoes and his trousers from the waist down were stained blue from the lake muck.

The Pavilion of Beautiful Views, painted on an islet in the middle of the west lake, overlooks the whole water park. Tourists cross the bridge for the view and the rats slide between the lattice in search of morsels under the pavilion porch.

"Rat islet to me," said the hunter.

"Why rats?"

"The government cadre offered me pigs, rats, or plastics," he said between slow rows, "so, be honest with me now, what would you choose?"

"Economics."

"Listen, fine shoes for children come from these hides, and we marinate the meat in ginger, pepper, and brine, and then the meat is pressed, dried, and recooked with sesame seed oil. Some of the pancake vendors on the street serve barbecued rat."

"Rattail economics."

"Pigs eat the rest," he said and rowed to the western side of the water park. Sandie tied the boat to a small pavilion near shore, shouldered his rifle and the blood soaked bundle of rats, and waddled over a low embankment.

Griever, mottled with blood and blue mud, followed the rat hunter into the trees. He folded his right ear, turned a strand of hair, and watched the animals wheedled behind the moist bushes; thousands of white moths lifted from broad leaves and lightened his volant shadow. Small birds healed the wild air he breathed, and wild flowers tousled on the paths to the golden pavilions. There, on a natural mount, a cleared circle in the polished trees, the hunter dressed the rats and spread the narrow hides on fine rosewood frames that enclosed a brick hearth. The trickster undressed down to his holster and underwear and spread his clothes on the same frames; then he followed the hunter to a narrow levee over a wide moat.

Matteo Ricci scratched the hard berm.

Obo Island bears three maidenhair trees, one white willow, four small brick houses, a concrete water ditch, a stone shrine and red banner near the levee, five humans, seventeen sows, three breeder boars, one wide barrow, several unnamed shoats and runners and a basketball court.

Obo, a tribal word that means "cairn," a tribal place where shamans gather and dream, is shaped the same as the nation, sheared and cleaved on two mounts. The nar-

164

row levee is a stem connected to the curved base of the island. The trees and houses are enclosed in a greater wall, and the wall separates the swine from the shaded courts on the eastern shore where the moat widens and pours into a deep lake. When the moon is new, the dark cold water heaves back the voices of dead miners, voices from an old lode that flooded at the end of the revolution.

Shitou, the stone man, was one of the few survivors when the dike collapsed and flooded the mine. Too old to find a new work place he made the island his home. Others, lost and dissociated in the revolution, curious and nonesuch wanderers, arrived and declared a new sericulture, swine, stone, birth control, and rat production unit, named Minus Number One.

Pigsie, denounced as a bourgeois nuisance, crossed the levee with two Hampshire gilts and a Spotted Poland China boar. Several months later he traded one Seghers, a new lean breed, for three common Yorkshires; then an agri-business consultant, secret agent and swine runner, traded a smart Duroc, which he named China Red, and one American Landrace for numerous concessions on the island. Nothing was conceded, however, because the runner was detained for bestialities. Communist cadres discovered the island and demanded a share of the swine herd for their silence and protection.

Kangmei circled the island in her prairie schooner for several weeks with moth seeds in small bundles under her arms; she watched the stone man break stones into laughter and the herder teach the swine to shoot baskets. The island, she decided, would be her place because it turned the revolution and the state into wild comedies. She crossed the levee with Yaba Gezi, the mute pigeon, late one winter night when the snow was pale blue.

Sandie, the most earnest and courteous of the wanderers, was the last to muster the swine on the island. He delivers

165

rat hides to the government, barters the marinated meat at the free market, and attends stone breaks and silk worms in the summer.

Griever held his breath on the levee to beat the smell of swine urine; he broke from the cloud of white moths at one end of the chine and burned his nostrils at the other end near the stone cairns. The trickster was silent and curious; he wandered over the island, down the greater wall, over the mounts, bowed, smiled, courted a cat and some mongrels, and shunned the torrid insects near a basketball court where he encountered the last character from the comic opera.

Pigsie, the lascivious peasant with huge golden hands, dribbled a basketball in a wide circle and then pitched it to the trickster at the back of the court. The athlete wore red shoes, loose shorts, knee pads, and a white mask to filter the dust raised by the swine.

Griever held the ball in silence and scratched the nubs with his thumbnails; a thin patch of mud broke and scattered. Swine urine burned his cheeks, ears, the thin skin on the back of his knees, and inner thighs. He bounced the ball once, twice, three times, and moved closer to the basket, which had been lowered for the swine. When three sows and a barrow snorted and wheeled in his direction, he leaped clean over the cairn into a vegetable garden that bordered the court and the greater wall.

"Pass ball, yes," cried Pigsie.

"Sooeeee," the trickster intoned and pitched the ball to the eager swine at the side of the court. *Rawrk, rawrk,* sounded a sow and nosed the ball down the sidelines; she thrust her wet snout high and bounced the ball to a boar near the basket. The swine had the same common character painted on their hams, tender loins, and picnic shoulders.

Matteo Ricci bounced on the back of the boar.

Pigsie blocked the pass, turned, dribbled low, and hooked

166

a basket. *Waaagghh, waaagghh,* the boar warned at the back court. The eager shoats imitated the wild sound and the cock crowed with pleasure.

"What do those characters mean?"

"Names, yes."

"Pig, hog, what?"

"No, no, Horse, Horse," said the herder.

"Wait a minute," said the trickster with his thumb on his ear, "the common character on the ass of that sow means 'horse'?"

"Yes, yes, *ma* means 'horse.'"

"Translate the other characters then."

"Little one named Ant," the swine herder explained, "*ma yi* means 'ant,' *ma* tones change, yes?" He smiled, pitched the ball to an eager shoat, and then faced the trickster.

"Name that one over there."

"Sacrifice."

"What kind of name is that?"

"Two characters mean 'horse' and 'omen,' yes."

"What about the sow under the basket?" The trickster pointed with one hand and then the other. "One character means 'horse,' what does the other character mean?"

"Jade."

"So, how does that translate then?"

"China Red named Agate, yes."

"Horse and jade make an agate," said the trickster, and he pointed to a couchant barrow in the center of the court. "No horse character on that one, no *ma* tone there, what is his name?"

"Mao Zedong."

"No shit, and a barrow no less."

"Communist cadres eat leader," he said, and then explained that the name was painted on the hams of those swine demanded by the cadres each month as tribute.

167

"What do you eat then?"

"Chicken."

"Lin Biao capon?"

"No, no, rooster," said Pigsie. He pinched the ball with his huge hands, dribbled around Mao Zedong, leaped over the barrow and shot a basket.

"Where clothes?"

"Muddied."

"Sandie, he rat man here."

"Where is here?"

"Obo hai dao, 'cairn island,'" he said and then bounced the ball to the boar with the blue ears and narrow rooter. The boar snouted the ball, *hummphhh, hummphhh,* from the back court and swished a basket, but the herder called a foul.

"Obo where?"

"Obo hai dao China."

"Hog heaven," Griever moaned and rolled his head from side to side. China Red and the shoats turned and stared at the naked trickster over the cairn. The fouled boar sat tight under the basket with his ears turned forward.

"Me live Albuquerque?"

"New Mexico?"

"Me live Albuquerque," said the cumbrous swine herder near the basket. The shoats faced the same direction, minded the boar, the ball, and the cock on the run.

"You were a student then?"

"America big tits," said the herder and passed the ball to the boar but a sow with butterflies painted on her ears intercepted with her snout high and made a basket.

"That she does," responded the trickster over the cairn. The manure on the garden parched his bare feet but he smiled and applauded the score.

"Studied aeronautic engineer."

"Albuquerque?"

168

"Balloons, little planes over desert, yes," he explained with a smile. His mouth spread like a marine animal, twice as wide as the words he practiced; his teeth were even, clean, and enormous. The herder summoned forbearance with his wide mouth, huge hands, feral toes, brows, and hunched shoulders; and he teased women to understand his unwonted burdens, the billow of his stout penis under denim.

"Ultralights?"

"Yes, yes, ultralights."

"Well, an ultralight was shipped to me here," said the trickster with his hands packed under the elastic band of his underwear. "So, when the plane is delivered, no more crowded train stations for me."

Pigsie told the trickster that basketball carried him from the rice brigades to teams in the cities, and then he was selected to be educated overseas in the operation of ultralight airplanes. Five months later, however, his student visa was withdrawn because, the investigation revealed, he touched the breasts of nineteen women at the International Adobe Basketball tournament; ten blondes, three were exposed. There, he pleaded, breasts were advertised, oversized, nurtured in the sun, oiled on the side, boosted on the seams; and pushed into common conversations, even on the run, and so, the athlete said, "So, so, bounced big tits on bleachers, yes."

"From ultralights to pigs?"

"Too much tits, so cadres said, pigs, rats, or plastics," he said and leaped over the cairn into the tomatoes and green beans. "So, which one you me choose?"

"Tits," cried the trickster.

"Pigs, no more tits."

"Rats were taken, right?"

"Right."

"Who has plastics?"

169

"Shitou."

"The stone man is here?"

"Right, right, right," he repeated over and over, stuck on a word that he seldom heard on the island. "Stone man, you meet him where, when he live in California?"

"When did he live there?"

"Build railroad," said the herder, "stone man build cold mountain railroad with hands down." He pushed the white mask back on his head, brushed the dust from his shoes, and wiped his hands on his shorts.

"Gold mountain, but he's not that old."

"Yes, cold," said the herder with a smile, and then he roamed with the swine down to the mount and the greater wall that enclosed the stone houses.

Shitou hunkered over mah jongg moves in the shadow of the maidenhair trees. The stone man turned a bamboo tile, and the trickster trod on the broken stones closer to the game. Three others shared the board and turned the seasons in silence.

Yaba Gezi, the mute pigeon, hovered in blue light.

Kangmei, the moth walker, was shrouded in silk.

Sandie matched a wind tile and cleaned his teeth with a blunt stick; he leaned to the side on the barrel of his rifle. Pleased with chance, he broke the silence and proposed that the faces of rats and bourgeois tourists become the suits. The trickster laughed but no one else was amused.

Matteo Ricci cracked maidenhair seeds.

Griever hesitated on the stone breaks that lined the path to the table beneath the trees; uncertain, he leaned back on his bare heels and bounced his toes together but the scene in the shadows outrode his imagination. He remembered blue bones, the prairie schooner, the black opal, and the birchbark manuscript. He twisted a wild hair on his right temple to catch the reason but the smell of swine urine rent the center of his dreams; his nose burned, he sneezed and lost his balance on the stones.

"Griever needs a mirror," said Sandie.

"No, no, but where are my clothes?"

"Your clothes are on the rosewood frames with the rat skins, remember?" Sandie clicked two red dragons, honor tiles, and explained to the trickster that his clothes, at least, would smell less of swine when he returned to the guest house with his stories.

Matteo Ricci strutted on the table.

Shitou leaned forward in silence, his back to the swine court and the levee. The greater wall ascended from the water like a stone serpent, a tribute to the dead miners, and widened near the mount. The stone man tended the bamboo and character suits; he smiled when the trickster moved closer on the breaks.

"Shitou, break me a stone."

"Shitou, *mo shu*," said the stone man.

"Stone what?"

"He said *mo shu*, 'magic,'" said Kangmei.

"Teach me the stone tricks," he pleaded on the new breaks, "show me how to shatter stone, like you did at the free market." The trickster tiptoed under the maidenhair trees.

"Sun Wukong, *mafan, mafan*," said the stone man. His wide simian ears beckoned when he moved his mouth; he whispered to the cock and smiled at the trickster.

"Mind monkey, what else?"

"Trouble, trouble," Kangmei translated.

"Trouble, no one would be here without trouble," said the trickster. He leaned back on a maidenhair tree, unholstered his scroll, and outlined parts of the swine islanders on the rough paper. The stone man was an ear, the moth walker a cocoon, the swine herder a penis, the rat hunter a mouth, and the mute pigeon a blue stone. In the

171

scenes that followed, these faces and other features became
stones in the greater wall at the mount. He traced enormous fish beached on the levee; moths, with wild silk banners raised over the blue stones, touched the earlier scenes
in the water park where the panda masturbated, and soldiers bound their feet.

"Deep inside the stone is a bird and humor," said the
stone man to the trickster. He moved a bench closer to the
maidenhair tree and placed one round stone on the rim.
"Dream that your hand moves back in time to when the
stone was formed," he said with his right hand poised over
the stone. "Dream that your hand moves to block the cold,
the cold that comes to the stone and laughter, and release
that little bird with the break." The trickster mocked the
stone man, hacked the stone twice, and bruised his hand.

"Show me the trick," said the trickster.

"Breath, hold that bird on your breath," said the stone
man with his hands on his smooth round stomach. He
leaned closer to the bench and broke two more slivers from
the stone.

"Bird breath, there, how is that?"

"Stomach, not your chest."

"Right, bird breath, stomach," mocked the trickster.

"*Dan tian*, 'inhale,' remember the bird."

"Concentrate, right?"

"*Yeren*," muttered the stone man.

"What was that?"

"Wildman," said the moth walker.

The mute pigeon appeared with two round mirrors, one
in each hand. He circled the trickster several times and
reined his image closer to the stone; his nose wobbled in
the mirrors and turned blue. The greater wall, the trees,
the cock, the swine behind the mount, the bird on his
breath, reeled in blue.

Griever remembered his dream in the shaman mirrors,

172

the heat, stubborn mosquitoes on the balcony, and the pictures of swine and blue bones. "Listen," he said as he turned to blue stone in the mirrors, "who was that man behind the evil mask, the one who held the blue bones?"

"Egas Zhang," whispered the moth walker.

"Egas Zhang," the others repeated, and the mute pigeon moved in silence. The mirrors trembled and the trickster lost his image.

"He was never, never my father," cried the moth walker. She lowered the shroud and pitched her head to the side, an instinctive gesture. Under the silk burnoose, she wore a thick turtleneck, the color of cedar bark, and loose pleated trousers that were open at the crotch like those of a child.

"No shit, and blond hair to prove it," said the trickster, closer to familiar seams and testaments. He winked twice, inhaled the noisome scent of swine, spread his chest, and strutted toward the mah jongg table. He wore nothing more than white underwear stained with blue mud on the crotch and his leather holster.

"Battle Wilson," she said through her clean hands, "he was my real father, born in the mountains." She crouched behind the table and twisted her slender waist to the right when she listened. She wore cloth shoes and bound her ankles with silk ribbons.

"Cold mountain?"

"Oklahoma."

"Did he give you an ancient manuscript?"

"Mountain View, Oklahoma."

"Tell me," the trickster crooned, "what did the scroll tell about the future, how can we live forever?" Griever planted his elbows on the table and studied the seasons, the winds, and the dragons. He leaned closer and waited to learn the secrets of the immortal bears from the mountains.

173

Kangmei turned to the side; she listened to the trickster and studied the puckers and wild creases on his cheeks when he smiled, but she would never answer his questions. Vital energies, she learned from the blind woman in the park, breed and mature in silence.

Yaba Gezi moved the mirrors and his mouth; he turned several words over in silence. The trickster leaned closer, listened to his breath, admired his own brows in the mirrors, and then he demanded a total translation of the silence.

"Nothing," said the moth walker to the mirrors.

"There, he made the same words."

"Children in the pond," she translated.

"What does that mean?"

"Blue bones are children in the pond," she said.

"Crosstalkers," said the trickster, bored with the silence and translation. The tiles wobbled and the winds turned when he crossed his bare legs and hit the table with his hands.

Pigsie, meanwhile, donned a wide peasant hat and packed four sucklings in the wicker baskets on the rear of his bicycle, two on each side, and pedaled once around the trees.

"Birth control," said Sandie.

"So what," answered the trickster.

"You were about to ask me about the sucklings."

"Birth control?"

"Women who nurse seldom get pregnant," the rat hunter explained, "and, so, the little swine get fed at the same time."

"Hard on nipples."

"We pull their teeth, perfect suckers."

"But why the pigs?"

"China is a one-child nation."

"Pigsie could suck, we could suck."

174

"Never," said Sandie.

"Our teeth?"

"No, we would get too fat."

"Chinese pragmatists in wicker baskets," the trickster said. "Listen, we could share the best tits on the route," he tendered, "and we might share much more than that and have a no-child nation, how about that?"

"Pigsie, remember, had too much tit."

"Leave the tits to me then," said the trickster.

"There was a teacher who tried that once," the rat hunter related, "he watched the suckers and snorted at women in his classes. Then he gave his clothes away, sucked several breasts for favors, the ultimate spiritual pollution, and was reeducated at a mental hospital."

"Porcine pollution."

"Our mental doctors never see sex as a problem here," the rat hunter construed, "so the poor man had to invent four new critical modernizations before he was released."

"Rats, pigs, plastics, and what else?"

"No, he proclaimed that transportation was limousinized, food was banquetized, clothes were westernized, and the nation was pavilionized."

The mute pigeon wheeled two hand mirrors from the shadows inside the stone house. Wild blue lights bucked the trickster over the threshold, pale spheres and nooses bounced on the back walls and ceiling. The room was decorated with old armor and hand weapons. Mao masks and several manikins held the margins of the room; and one papier-mâché monster loomed alone near a narrow window.

"Egas Zhang," shouted the trickster.

"We made his face with toilet paper," said the stone man when he removed the round mask from the monster. The paper face had been skewered and one ear was broken.

Matteo Ricci shivered at the window.

Griever marched closer to the monster; nose to nose, he reached to touch the blue bones when a light burst from the mute pigeon, circled the room, and the bones vanished. Bewildered, the trickster punched the evil monster hard in the stomach, two inches below the navel, and cracked the toilet paper and plaster cast.

Chinese hand weapons, hammers, battle axes, halberds and swords were stacked on crude museum tables. Spears with bright plumes and tassel ornaments were mounted on the back wall. Breastplates and rhinoceros hide armor covered the manikins in the corners. Outside, at the back of the stone house, there were ballistae and a cloud ladder near the narrow swine houses.

Griever climbed the ladder, whistled to the swine on the other side of the greater wall, and then he returned to the museum. He wielded each weapon on the museum tables, admired a jade mace, an axe head, and then, in a sudden ritual maneuver, he raised a broad sword, roared, and cleaved the monster down the middle. Egas separated and stood on plastic shoes for a few seconds; then the parts, paper nostrils, narrow chest, and hollow testicles, toppled over. Crepe paper funeral flowers, the core of the monster, eased open on the cold concrete.

"Egas Zhang the eunuch," cried the moth walker.

"Pig feed."

"No swine would have him," she cursed.

"Shit paper then," said the trickster near the window. He wiped the blade clean, returned the sword to the table, and picked a bouquet of flowers from the remains.

Kangmei leaned over from the waist to break parts from the head of the monster. Her rich blond hair brushed the broken chest and paper head as she turned. When the others returned to mah jongg, the trickster moved closer to the moth walker, to the swell of her thighs; he thrust his hand between the pleats in her trousers and touched her moist crotch. She struggled to escape his wild hands. His penis leaped from his underwear and bounced on her bare buttocks; she lost her balance and tumbled forward on the divided monster. The trickster lost flesh and bruised his penis on the broken cast.

ℭ Duck Webs

Mikhail Markovich Borodin was once known as the Emperor of Canton. He was born a Russian, enlisted in the Jewish Social Democratic Bund, and founded a school for emigrant children in the slums of Chicago; then, dashed in radical journalism, he became a miscued courier in communism.

Borodin carried out the policies of Joseph Stalin and was heaved to the side in a peasant revolution. Now, two generations later, Canton has become Guangzhou, a new free market ordeal, and the old peasant radicals are reborn as clever corporate capitalists. Where the missionaries strained to save the souls of heathens in wild histories, the capitalists now search for new consumers to rule; plastics, perfumes, aphrodisiacs, washing machines are advertised on state television.

Mikhail Borodin arrived at the round table with a small and silent woman. The cadres were captivated by his voice and dark eyes, his personal charm, and venture capital. He wore a loose summer suit and a scarlet necktie decorated with golden cranes, a crest similar to the martlet. He closed his hands when he spoke, never clenched, and opened them when he listened.

"Mikhail Borodin?" said the trickster.

"Grusenberg," he said with his hands closed, "and who

might you be, sir?" Dark blue veins swelled on the back of his pale open hands.

"Griever de Hocus."

"De Hocus," he parried with his hands closed, "you would not be the first person to observe a likeness to Mikhail Borodin."

"Must have been the footless ducks."

"Cranes, sir."

"Whatever, the crest on your imperial tie."

"The Chinese must appreciate your humor," he teased and then opened one hand to touch his thick black moustache. Dubious of the match, he invited interruptions.

"Where is home?"

"I was born in the winter, and we live in the summer," he intoned from a distance, "but what would you do with such facts?"

"Borodin said he was born in snow and lived in the sun, and what good are facts," the trickster responded with his thumb on his ear.

"Fanya, this is Mister de Hocus," he said to the woman at his side. She bowed in silence and then moved to the other side of the table with the elder cadres.

"Honored guests, friends, comrades, the anniversary of the founding of the People's Republic of China is coming at a time when the Chinese people have achieved new successes of socialist construction of the four modernizations," said Li Rui-Huan, the mayor of Tianjin, at a reception and dinner held in the ballroom of the Friendship Club.

"Not in alarm clocks," mumbled Colin Gloome. He leaned closer to the cadre at one of the head tables and complained about several inferior clocks he had purchased and then returned to a local department store. He doubled the *mao tai* toasts, the white-lightning of the middle world.

"What brand?" asked one cadre who wore two red rib-

179

bons on his tunic. Translators roamed between the round tables to harvest information, serve the curiosities of the visitors, and to preserve their elder cadres.

"Panda, dead ones."

"Gloome, those panda hands turn on communist time, the same clocks were returned with the same alarms," said the trickster who landed at the same table with Gloome, Michael Grusenberg and his wife Fanya, several senior cadres, and a vacant seat. Hannah Dustan, Carnegie Morgan, and the other teachers were seated at the two nearest tables.

"This evening, the presence of our foreign friends brings us friendship and joy, and adds color to the festival," the mayor continued from behind a polished podium. He wore a tailored suit and vest, a serious businessman with a paunch, while the elder cadres at the round tables were dressed in tunics and appeared wiser behind their practiced smiles.

"Now, allow me, on behalf of the Tianjin Municipal People's Government, to convey our warm welcome and sincere gratitude to all foreign experts, teachers, engineers, technicians, administrative staff members, representatives of foreign companies, and other foreign friends as well as their spouses present at this reception. . . ."

"Slaves, not teachers," muttered Morgan.

"No speech, time to eat," hinted Hannah, "that revolution is over over here." She waved a dark cigarette and when she leaned forward to whisper or listen, the cadres and their eager translators minded her breasts behind wide linen puckers and balloon sleeves. "Look at that table, the entremets, rich dishes, but right now liver and onions would do me fine, even a rare burger on white bread."

The Friendship Club was established by the British during the concessions period. From Victoria Park the colonists wound down Race Course Road to the club which is located near the new simulated water park. The racecourse and horse stables were ruined; but the revolution reserved the vast gardens, mature roses, marble columns, polished colonial beams, billiard rooms, mineral baths, and other recreational immunities for the elder cadres. The Red Guards caused more harm to religious monuments, the noses and arms of statues in wood and stone, than to colonial structures.

"The People's Republic of China has gone through its eventful existence for thirty-four years. Although there have been all kinds of obstacles and difficulties in our way, we have achieved tremendous successes in both socialist revolution and socialist constructions," the mayor lectured with his head down.

"Soviet toilets leak in the guest house," said the trickster to the woman who had arrived late, "the good mayor must mean socialist misconstruction."

"No squat," she whispered and then pinched her mouth closed to hold back laughter. She winked at two cadres on the other side of the table and brushed her short sorrel hair with her hands.

The capacious round tables bordered the buffet where waiters delivered culture in garnished cuisines: the *cai*, fish, pork, chicken, venison, duck webs, pheasant, tendons; and the *fan*, rice, millet, maize, buckwheat, noodles, beans; and cabbages, turnips, mushrooms, peaches, pears, oranges; and mountain haw, red pepper, ginger, garlic, scallion; and cinnamon and litchi, in numerous gastronomic combinations; and borrowed cuisines, apple strudel and ice cream with chocolate, but never sweet potatoes because the smell reminded the old cadres of the peasant revolution. The mayor lectured, the cadres smiled, the teachers whispered and wrote notes on paper napkins.

"Who the devil are you?"

"Sinologue opposed to golden lilies," she wrote on the

back of a napkin. She printed over two words because the paper had blotted.

"Same here," he whispered.

"Who is the same?"

"Griever de Hocus," he printed in block letters. Others at the table were distracted, so he raised the unfolded napkin to his chest.

"Alicia Little," she whispered in his ear.

"Wait a minute," he mumbled.

"Founder of the Natural Foot Society."

"Never," he wrote on the napkin.

"Why never?"

"Too much cleavage," he wrote and then drew a silhouette of a woman with enormous breasts. She watched his hands move on the paper and then she folded her arms over her chest.

"What do you know about missionaries?"

"My grandmother," said the trickster.

"Where?"

"House at the Little Crossroads."

"Lottie Moon?"

"Lottie Moon de Hocus."

"No, where was she born then?"

"Virginia," he whispered, "with no cleavage, and then the Southern Baptist Convention paid her fare to the North China Mission where she was creased with loneliness."

"Lottie Moon is a distant relative of mine," she whispered with enthusiasm, even closer to the ear of the trickster. "She had much cleavage, but where did you learn about missionaries?"

"Alicia Little," he wrote on a second napkin, "no cleavage either, but she had natural feet." The trickster had moved closer to touch her mouth when she whispered in his ear. He watched her breasts rise and her hands move on

182

the rim of the table. She wore a thin gold band on her little finger.

"Relative?"

"No, my friend binds her feet and is writing a book about the Natural Foot Society," the trickster whispered, "have you ever bound your feet?"

"No, who is she?"

"China," he wrote on the napkin.

"No squat."

"China Browne."

"Nineteen tables and the last chair is next to you," she whispered with a smile. "Even so, you make more sense than the mayor right now."

"What is your real name?"

"Sammie Moon," she wrote on a napkin.

"No shit?"

"Lottie Moon was right, you know."

"About what?"

"Missionaries who wear Chinese clothes lose the power of protest, manly protest against evil," she whispered in short phrases.

"What about clowns?"

"The present political and economic situation in our country is excellent," the mayor continued his lecture with his hands in his pockets. "The political stability and unity have become an irreversible historical trend. . . ."

"No shit," whispered Carnie.

"The financial and economic situation is steadily improving. New priority projects have started as planned. The causes of science, culture, education, sports, and sanitation are prosperously developing. The peoples life has been greatly improved. . . ."

"Who cleans the toilets?" mumbled Carnie.

"The smell of shit in the classroom building is too much," moaned Hannah. She pinched her nose and two translators rushed to her side to construe that natural urge in a crowded nation.

"Listen," she whispered to the translators, "no flush, no excusee, my stomach needs food, no more fecal politics." She leaned forward to light a cigarette, a measured move, and smiled at the translators. "Could you little dears hustle me some munchies?"

"Munchies?"

"Bagels and cream cheese."

"Me too, make that two," pleaded Carnie.

"Please write," said the translator.

"Two bagels, dough, with a hole," she said and then drew a picture on a napkin. "Bagel, no doughnut, but on second thought even a plastic doughnut would do."

"Bagel, bagel, plastic doughnut," repeated the embarrassed translator. His cheeks burned when he examined the picture on the napkin.

"*Goubuli bu kong,*" whispered Carnie. The translators covered their mouths and the cadres at that side of the table smiled to be polite.

"What does that mean?" asked Hannah.

"Stuffed bun with no hole."

"Listen, the mayor imagines a nation of computers," she muttered with two lighted cigarettes, two more moves to control the conversation, "when our students have yet to meet a real vacuum cleaner and electric can opener." She moved to her right, closer to the cadre with red ribbons on his tunic and told stories about how poor his people were dressed, and how so much dust would ruin the computers, and about the loathsome smell of shit in the classrooms. "Chinese shit has permeated my fine woolens and diskettes, terrible, terrible." The two translators followed her words with political imagination, and the other cadres were amused while he watched her sleeves open and close.

"Forget the bagel," mocked Morgan.

"I mean, how can these people move into computers," she carped in a cloud of smoke, "when they still play 'Jingle Bells' and 'White Christmas' in the summer?"

"Listen to the lyrics."

"In the field of foreign relations," the mayor emphasized through his translator, "we have enhanced the self-reliance and strengthened the unity and cooperation with the third world countries as well as all friendly countries, leading to the promotion of friendship between the peoples of all countries. All this shows that the prospect of our socialist construction is utterly bright, and there is great hope for the revitalization of the Chinese people."

"Evil Egas," the trickster wrote on a napkin.

"What does that mean?"

"Egas Zhang, on the other side of the table, the one with the cigarette near his cheek," he wrote in a curve at the corner of the paper. The napkin was covered with conversations.

"So what?"

"Listen," the trickster warned in a whisper from the side of his mouth, "his bamboo brain is about to open like a bird cage."

"Please, no more show for me," she pleaded, and then wrote the same words on a napkin. "Wait, you can eat too much later, or climb a tree, or something else to impress me, but not now, please."

"Egas is a rare bird," the trickster whispered, and then on a clean napkin he wrote that he intended to examine the mayor on the future of blacks and minorities. The message was passed to the other side of the table.

Egas read the note on the napkin and was at the side of the trickster with a wide and nervous smile. "Mister Griever," he whispered, his breath sour with nicotine, "mayor is very busy man with new water project for city, maybe later you could meet the mayor."

"What about minorities?"

"Minorities liberated," he insisted.

"What about blacks?"

"What black?"

"The African students," the trickster whispered over his shoulder, "we must ask the mayor about the segregation of the black students on campus."

"No segregation," he rasped and smiled in a cloud of cigarette smoke, "no prejudice since revolution."

"What about the Algerian watchmakers?"

"Mayor answer questions later."

"Chinese women are not allowed to see the watchmakers or the blacks," said the trickster in a louder voice. "Egas, do you know the answer to that question?"

"Mister Egas," she summoned in a whisper and at the same time kicked the trickster on the shins when she turned to shake hands. "Sammie Moon is my name, thank you for inviting me to this dinner and celebration of the revolution."

"Yes, yes, thank you," he responded and held her cool hand. He turned his back to avoid the trickster and invited her to visit his office and the new addition to the university library where she would discover material on missionaries. Her thighs opened as she turned on the chair.

"Watchmakers?" she wrote on a napkin.

"Algerians, stranded at guest house, no money, no watches to repair," the trickster printed in small block letters. "African students stranded too, their governments overthrown, no homeland, no women, so the watchmakers and the blacks dance together at parties."

"Third world time?"

"New China, since the revolution, said Zhou Enlai, has not practiced any discrimination," the trickster wrote on a napkin.

"Incredible."

186

"Would you like to tour my flush toilet?" Griever whispered closer to her ear, and their shoulders touched; her neck and cheeks blushed.

"Like the whole country, the city of Tianjin has made great achievements in every field. As you can see yourselves, the face of the city has greatly changed during the past few years. The completion of the water project will not only profoundly affect the economic development and the people's life of Tianjin, but also greatly stimulate people's socialist enthusiasm in our construction. . . ."

"Not to mention the taste of the water," the trickster muttered, "we were told to pan our bath water for lead and other valuable metals."

"Who is the moustache?"

"Where?"

"Near Egas," whispered Sammie.

"Mikhail Borodin."

"Please," she wrote on a napkin.

"Michael Grusenberg and Fanya Orluk."

"Who is he?"

"Spy," the trickster printed.

"Never mind."

"He bottles wine and shampoo."

"Right."

"Cover stories," whispered the trickster. "Watch his hands open and close, he must have his paws into power, nuclear weapons." He touched her shoulder once more.

"Watch your hands," she warned.

"Give me a chance."

"You are a chance," she whispered, but at a distance from his ear. "Once more, who is that woman over there, she must be a translator?"

"Hester," the trickster whispered, "marvelous, but what on earth is she doing here?" He was surprised, turned on his chair, and turned his thumb on one ear.

"Who is she?"

"Hester Hua Dan," he whispered with his hands in nervous motion, "she's a translator, the daughter of some government official."

"She's been watching you."

"Why not?"

"We are deeply convinced that the city of Tianjin will be built in the near future into a modern industrial and commercial city with beautiful environment and with prosperity in economy and culture as well as an important international commercial port.

"We can never forget the assistance and support given by our foreign friends in our socialist construction. Over the years, the foreign experts, teachers, engineers, technicians . . . representatives of foreign companies who are working in Tianjin have achieved remarkable successes and played a positive role in raising our city's scientific and technical level, in training qualified personnel in all fields, and in promoting economic and technical cooperation and exchange with foreign countries," the mayor lectured through his translator.

"I love children," Gloome announced to the local head of the Communist Party on his left. The cadre smiled, nodded, but remained silent. "Ask him to ask me why I love children," he said to the translator who appeared near his shoulder.

"We are pleased that you love children," the translator whispered in response. "Chinese people love children."

"Today the president made a decision," Gloome continued to speak to the translator. He downed more *mao tai* and stretched the loose skin on his cheeks and chin.

"What president?"

"President of the United States," he commanded with the peevish manner of an alcoholic. "He ordered a thousand more nuclear weapons to burn children."

188

"Chinese people love children," the translator whispered, "we do not understand." He wore a diplomatic smile while he perspired under the pressure. The cadre understood what the barbarian said, but he held his distance and advantage with a translator.

"American workers have cars and telephones," Gloome muttered to one side and then the other. "Chinese, what do they have?"

"We have foreign experts," said the translator.

"Nothing but dust, not even an alarm clock that works," he pouted, downed a *mao tai*, and then he invited the translator closer, "but tell me, do you know where a man can find a good plastic surgeon?"

"Soon, we eat dinner."

"We will, as always, make our own contributions to promote harmony among the peoples of the world, to oppose hegemony and to safeguard world peace. We sincerely hope that every foreign friend working in Tianjin will continue friendly cooperation with us," the mayor recited from the podium. "May I ask our foreign friends to forgive us for any inconveniences in the working and living conditions during your stay in Tianjin. We will make every effort to improve these conditions as well as our work."

Hester printed three words on thin paper, and then she asked Li Wen to deliver the note to the trickster on the other side of the ballroom.

Griever was slow to unfold the note. He cleared his throat and prepared to read, unaware that others at the table watched his moves, curious to discover a clue to the contents. With his fingers, he teased the words beneath the last thin fold, like a breast under coarse cotton. He turned, peeled the words, blushed, and pushed his thumb hard on his ear; and then, he leaped from his chair.

Sammie Moon leaned closer to read the words on the thin paper, as she had done when the trickster wrote to her on napkins, and then she turned in the other direction. She was embarrassed, surprised at her own mien and mood, cornered in the outrageous presence of the trickster and his rash of intimacies.

"I am pregnant," were the three words printed on the note. The words were exposed to view on the table, on a mound of other words, and notes, written on napkins. The trickster had been too casual with the message.

"Now, I'd like to propose a toast to the thirty-fourth anniversary of the founding of the People's Republic of China," the mayor said and raised his glass, "to the revitalization of the Chinese people, to the harmony and friendship between the Chinese people and all peoples of the world, to expressing our thanks for the help received from foreign friends, to the health of all friends and comrades present at this reception, cheers."

"Cheers."

"Marvelous, listen," the trickster pleaded when he found her near the door at the back of the ballroom, "I've got a perfect plan."

"No plan, no, no," she chanted. Hester was worried that someone would find them together. "You go back now, back to the table, no, no plan."

"Meet me at the movie tomorrow night," the trickster said, "we can work out the plans there, trust me, at the movie then."

"What plans?"

"Ultralight," he whispered and turned to the side.

"Ultralight what?"

"Yes," he said with pleasure.

"What is ultralight?"

"Small airplanes."

"No, no plans," she pleaded and pushed the trickster back into the ballroom, back from her memories. "Please, no plans, go, go now, go to eat."

190

"Tomorrow at the movie then, promise me."

"Yes, but no plans."

"This is marvelous," he whispered and then whistled as he danced between the round tables. When the mayor concluded with a *mao tai* toast, the teachers were driven with hunger to the front of the buffet line; five round tables with various regional cuisines.

Egas read the three words on the thin paper and discovered that his daughter had written the note to the trickster. His hands clenched, he shuddered and gathered the other notes on napkins before the trickster returned. Sammie remembered too late to recover the intimate message and the critical words she had written on the napkins.

❡ Outdoor Movies

The cicadas roared once the rainbow came down over the brick road behind the campus dormitories. Later, the wind crouched at broken windows; colors wavered, voices were hollow, and the last mosquitoes whined near the pond. Seven narrow banners in red and blue hues descended from a high wire between two buildings. The plastic rainbow marked the entrance to the outdoor movie theater.

The road narrowed to a turnstile under the rainbow. There, a woman with a disabled child directed admission once a week to the free movies. The dark woman and her child lived in an abandoned automobile.

Maosak, or "martial music," wailed and whistled from the thirteen loudspeakers on campus, a reminder that the movie would begin at dusk behind the concrete dormitories. The white cloth screen was stretched between two telephone poles; silent advertisements, pictures of plastics and aphrodisiacs, similar to those presented on state television, enlivened the material aspirations of those students who claimed the first rows on the bare beaten earth.

Griever circled the pond and tossed wads of *mantou* to the slow carp below the bridge; he spat and heard the cadence of soldiers. Opera music bounced low down the moat, echoed between constructions, and over the dead water. He renounced the carp and followed the students with their small benches and stools down the road to the outdoor movie. Secret societies marched to burn the missions; the trickster doubled his gait under the slack rainbow banner and outspanned the music.

The trickster meandered to the back of the court between the dormitories. He waved to his students on the aisles but never paused; he was too eager to meet Hester Hua Dan. He had prepared three nuptial stories: the first, the only one he would reveal at the movie that night, was an avian deliverance on an ultralight airplane; the second was diplomatic shelter; and the third, he would never even whisper, was capitulation to socialist bureaucracies. Abortion, however, never entered his mind.

"Professor Griever, please come to be here, we have seat," called a student near the center of the audience. "Come, we share seat." The trickster, encumbered with his name, pretended not to hear the loud invitation, but the student persisted and pushed down the uneven rows to practice casual conversation.

"Professor, nice and pleasant evening," he said with a smile that stretched his cheeks back to his ears. Nathan had studied several languages; he aspired to be a translator at a state tourist bureau. American tourism succeeds wild histories, he reasoned, because dollars are needed to purchase computers.

"Yes, indeed, but no breeze."

"Yes, yes, no breeze."

"Red Guard mosquitoes," said the trickster and brushed his neck and shoulders. He scratched two bites on his right elbow. "The vicious ones, so late in the season."

"Red Guard, that was a joke," said Nathan. He laughed, bowed, and clapped. "Yes, yes, mosquitoes too late at movie, very vicious, very good word," he said and cocked his head to the right. "Do you have vicious mosquitoes at your home?"

"American mosquitoes own television sets."

"Professor, you tell more jokes."

"What is the movie?"

"Very good movie," said the student, "story about women on train between Beijing and Shanghai." His cheeks shivered when he pronounced certain plosive sounds; the words were rushed, detonations in a sentence. When he listened he moved closer and whispered the words he heard. His mouth movements were echoes, unvoiced intimations, a hindrance to casual conversations. Echolalia, the trickster learned, was one name for the habit: the repetition of phrases spoken by others, an aphonic translation.

"Have you seen it?"

"What see?"

"The movie about trains."

"Yes, this movie, it was on the television some time," he said. Nathan, a name he adopted for the foreign teachers in the classroom, was lean, muscular, and intense. The veins on his neck doubled when he listened; one ear was notched like a farm animal. He nurtured a sheer moustache. The mosquitoes never bothered him when he was awake.

"Well, I look forward to seeing the movie for the first time," said the trickster and waved a mosquito down from his nose, "are there any sex scenes in the movie?"

"What, sex scenes?"

"Men, women, and passion."

"Sometimes," he blushed.

"Sometimes in the movies?"

"No, no," he said and doubled over with embarrassment and nervous laughter. "Never in our movies here."

"Where then, in secret magazines?"

"America, are there such movies there?" His hands and cheeks were calm and he listened with no repetition; he was hesitant to even whisper what he might hear about sex from a foreign teacher.

194

"There are movies that show everything," the trickster said and touched his ear, "nude men and women on screen, stunt cocks and cunties, animals on a wild mount, even mosquitoes in the forbidden act."

"Stunt cock and cunties," he whispered.

"Never mind."

"Stunt cock and cunties, these words are not in our dictionaries," the student complained. Nathan leaned closer and asked the trickster for a basic definition of the words. He printed the words in a notebook.

"Saved by the movie," the trickster said and searched the faces in the dark. The autumn mosquitoes were slow, but their bites burned on his neck and shoulders. On screen, two attractive women were about to begin their careers as state railway attendants.

"Professor," said a student from behind. "Griever, would that be proper to use your given name?" Faith, the name she had adopted for the foreign teachers, was the spoiled daughter of an important production cadre and a music teacher.

"You will like movie, goodbye," he said. Nathan was eager to leave, to avoid Faith, who, according to the other students, was a monitor, a devoted student propagandist, and an informer to the director of the foreign affairs bureau.

"Goodbye, Nathan."

"Must you leave?" asked Faith.

"Griever first, professor last," he mocked and continued to search the faces, "or, you could address me as Number One, like your factories and hotels."

"You look for someone tonight?"

"Hester Hua Dan, yes, do you know her?"

"Certainly," replied Faith, "she is well-known."

"Where?"

"Here, on our campus."

"What does she do on the campus?" the trickster asked, but he was hesitant to discuss his lover with a student informer.

"Well, her father is Egas Zhang."

"What?" he roared and wheeled his head and hands. He bowed and turned wild, not a dance but an unwise move to awaken a panic hole at the movies. Later, he would scream in the broad hole near the pond. "Hester and Kangmei are sisters," he strained to whisper.

"Why did you want her?"

"Egas Zhang, are you sure?"

"Yes, she admires her father."

"Fear is a much better description," he commanded.

"How do you know her then?"

"Do you?"

"My mother taught her music," said Faith.

"Music then," he muttered. Griever was not pleased that a student informer, who reported to the foreign affairs director, was so curious about his situation at the movie.

On screen, the women boarded the train. One woman was too proud; she worked hard to impress the cadres, but her vanities were uncovered and denounced. The woman blundered on the rails; she overcompensated with sunniness, passive mirth, and dedicated service, and was disabused by a drunken cadre.

"Was she to meet you?"

"No," the trickster lied with ease, "but she was a translator at the reception and dinner last night, and she asked me to find a word in my dictionaries."

"How interesting," said Faith.

"Yes."

"Griever, do you like teaching in our country?"

"Yes, very much," sighed the trickster.

"What word?"

"Well," he whispered and punched one ear, "*stool*

196

pigeon, she wanted to know the meaning of that expression because someone at the dinner table said some of the students were stool pigeons."

"Stool pigeons?"

"Will you see her soon?" asked the trickster.

"Yes, perhaps soon," she courted.

"Well, then perhaps you could tell her the definition of the expression," said the trickster with one hand posed on his cheek.

"Stool pigeon?"

"Yes, it means an alert and intelligent person who listens with great care and interest," the trickster recited. "Would you like me to repeat that?"

"Thank you, no, I understand."

"You, for example, are a stool pigeon," said the trickster in the dark. He turned to avoid the laughter that swelled in his stomach; he concentrated on his mother, aluminum, small women in motel rooms, the smell of swine urine, and the humor vanished. On screen, no one pitied the woman who lost her pride on the wild rails.

"No, not really, not me," pleaded Faith.

"*Stoolie* is the abbreviation."

"Stoolie?"

"Yes, and you are a stoolie."

"Yes?"

"Yes, for sure."

"Thank you, professor," she said with her hands folded behind her back. Faith bowed and returned to her rearward stool in the dark. The mosquitoes swarmed the trickster; he smiled, brushed his shoulders, and punched his ear once more. He raced back through his memories and conversations; back in wild dreams and crossed the border to uncover the catchwords, the leers and red letters that would reveal the connections between Egas Zhang and Hester Hua Dan.

Hester waited behind the screen near a statue of Zhou Enlai. The students surrounded the movie and watched from both sides of the screen. From behind, the images were blurred, reversed and more romantic in feathered colors; the woman and the passengers on the train spread over the faces, the weeds, and the bronze statue. White shirts held the rims of smiles, flower petals; an enormous nose and the mountains outside the window on the back of the screen roamed over cheeks and foreheads in the audience. The trickster walked down the aisle to the end of the train.

"Hester," he whispered from behind the statue. She stepped back into the shadow, turned to welcome his voice, but avoided his eager hands on her moist shoulders. She resisted his breath, lower moves, and reared back once more into a blurred scene from the movie.

"We must not be seen here," she cautioned.

"Come to my apartment."

"No, no, not allowed in the guest house."

"To the water park then."

"No, no, gate is closed at night."

"Come to the classroom then, we can be alone there," he insisted. Scenes from the movie beamed around them on both sides of the statue.

"No, no, locked."

"Locked, locked, what is not locked?"

"What do you want?"

"Behind the dormitories, we can sit in that old car with the vegetable garden under the hood," he whispered with enthusiasm and reached for her hands.

"No, no, must leave."

"Wait," the trickster pleaded and towed her back behind the statue and held her arms. "Tell me now, who is your father?"

"Egas Zhang," she whispered.

"Why is that a secret?"

"No, no."

"Tell me now."

"He hates foreigners, he never allows me to be in public, never with foreign teachers," she whispered and spread her back on the cool stone base of the statue.

"Does he hate me?"

"Yes, he reads mail from teachers," she said with her head on the stone. "Sometimes, he reads letters to us at home, and at meetings with workers in guest house," she recited. "He laughed when you write to woman, what was her name?"

"China Browne."

"Yes, yes, he read letter."

"Tomorrow, the customs cadres will inspect the ultralight airplane that was shipped to me, and then, we can fly out of this place forever," said the trickster with one hand raised near his ear. He moved closer, touched her thighs, and brushed mosquitoes from her swollen cheeks.

"No, no more plans."

"Macao, how does that sound?"

"No, no."

"Freedom on an ultralight."

"No, no airplane."

"Sandie will know how to bribe someone for a gasoline ration card," he whispered with his shoulder to the stone. "We can travel as diplomats, free as birds over the rice paddies."

"Griever, listen to me."

"Sure," he whispered close to her neck.

"Egas order me abortion."

"Never, never," the trickster bellowed behind the statue. He drew the attention of several students in the audience behind the screen. The woman in the movie rescued the evil cadre who had overeaten and lost his breath; howbeit, the man cursed her consideration when he recovered. The audience and the passengers on the train pardoned the woman her pride and railed at the debauched cadre, a vicious man. "No one steals our child in this world," he chanted but his voice was lost in the movie scene.

"He read napkins," she whispered.

"So what?"

"The napkins from the reception."

"Never mind," he whispered and held her close to his chest, "soon we will be as free as birds." Three mosquitoes marched down his moist arm, selected a rich vein between the thin hairs, and stung the trickster.

"Egas cursed me," she cried.

"The Marxmass Carnival, we can meet then," he said in search of solace and a place to remember. "Listen, meet me outside the guest house that night and the plans will be complete, we can leave from the guest house and spend the night on the island."

"No, no plans."

"We can fly out in the morning from the island."

"No, no, not now."

"Why not?"

"Never fly in airplane," she told the trickster but held back the real reason: her fear, resignation to paternal power, and her dedication to the nation.

"Never mind," the trickster murmured and pinched the blood fattened mosquitoes on his arm. "Macao is marvelous, we will be there soon, together, free as birds."

"Free as birds," she repeated in a whisper and wiped her cheeks with her hands. She smiled and touched his hands in the shadow of the statue.

The train on the back of the movie screen reached the final destination and the woman, the new attendant who overrode her pride for the socialist state, presented the evil cadre with a white rose. The passengers and the audience behind the screen applauded the paternalistic conclusion.

❡ Forbidden Cities

Maxim's de Paris was delivered in Beijing on the anniversary of the founding of the People's Republic of China.

Griever was there, dressed in his lemon raglan opera coat and pleated trousers to mock a precious moment in the wild histories of capitalism. He leaned back on a small tree, potted in concrete for the occasion, unholstered his scroll, and painted an ornate sedan chair raised on the fattened shoulders of missionaries, silhouettes with white masks on rough paper. The sedan was overturned in the second scene; peasants circled the chair and ate the missionaries.

Matteo Ricci scratched the side of the shoulder pack and pushed his head and one claw out between the folds; he shivered and thrust his beak at the figures on the rough paper. The trickster touched his wattles with blue paint and then rolled the paper back into his holster.

Griever holds cold reason and those unctuous word mongers who palm stories and passions on a lunge line when he paints the world. His imagination is a dance to discover interior landscapes; but now and then his trickeries on rough paper are cornered in popular clichés and institutions, abused by those who vest their personal power in labels and tickets to the main events. When this happens, when the world appears overused like a turnstile, he pleats and doubles shrouds and veronicas, creases photographs, folds brochures, dictionaries, and menus, to weaken the plane realities.

The trickster doubled the world the first time when he was nine; when a small woman who lived near the river in a house made of doors told him that the world flew on four folds. He folded paper airplanes from historical pictures at school, crenellated the presidents, creased birds and animals free; and then he painted over the pleats and seams. Some situations, however, demand more than paint and creases to understand the cultural calendars.

Pierre Cardin, the man behind Maxim's de Beijing, sailed in a wide circle under his red awnings; his image in four folds on a crosswind past the golden fleur-de-lis, stalled in flight between the double doors of his extravagant restaurant. The hat check woman, vernal child of peasants turned courtier, bound in a red and black uniform, tossed the paper capitalist back into the street; the creased announcement rubbed on the bricks at the feet of curious citizens. An astonished audience at the entrance witnessed the restoration of imperial palace operas.

Sammie Moon appeared with a tall blond man who wore a class necktie, a blue cashmere blazer, and narrow shoes with leather tassels. She turned and smiled at the entrance, the blond pursued, and the audience applauded their glissade on the carpet. Two doormen, restive in their pillbox hats and short red coats with golden epaulets, escorted the handsome couple to the spiral staircase and their high lunch. The new waiters were nervous, alert to seat the first customers.

The trickster brushed the wide sleeves of his opera coat and watched from the border. The audience praised the other pale actors who mounted the stairs, unaware that at the maiden performance one lunch on the imperial stage cost more than four months' salary of an average worker.

"So, so," said a man with a harsh voice, "so there is the

third forbidden city." He parked his imported bicycle with a diplomatic license at the curb behind the trickster.

"So, so," mocked Griever.

"What is that you have there?"

"Matteo Ricci."

"Surely, this is a day to remember," said the man with his leg over the center bar of the bicycle. "Mao Zedong, Pierre Cardin, and Matteo Ricci, the founders, all here at once."

"So, so, how time folds," said the trickster.

"Really," said the man with his nervous hands in his pockets, "may we ask then, who is your employer, restaurant or state?"

"Neither, imperial restorations."

"China was discovered twice on television and now the nation lives in three centuries at the same time," he said in a loud voice and snapped a rubber band on his thumb.

"Twice?"

"Once a series, twice a tour."

"Do you teach?"

"That much for the revolution," he sighed and brushed his coarse hair behind his ears. "The imperial palace, this forbidden franchise, but tell me, where are the residences of the government leaders?" The man did not wait for an answer, he mounted his bicycle and peddled down Qianmen Street toward Tiananmen Square.

Griever roamed between the bicycles to the red carpets at the entrance. He amused the audience with his opera turns, the movements of his head, a simian smile, the swathe of his hands and sleeves; he astonished the doormen, not with his wild clothes, but with his cock in a shoulder pack. The bright grapes doubled on the spiral stairs and oceans were becalmed on stained glass. Florid scenes bloomed on the windows; the red lasted and the blues wavered, illuminated from behind with fluorescence.

Solvents permeated the dark bar. The walls and varnished beams were embossed with *art nouveau* golden poppies, smartened with arabesques. The trickster leaped over a marble console table into the main dining room where three parties were seated.

"No, no, no," moaned Sugar Dee.

"Madam, your words are landscapes," the trickster said and pulled out a chair at their table. He moved the candleholders and lamp to the side, motioned to a waiter, ordered a menu, and a bowl of water for Matteo Ricci.

"Mister de Hocus, hear me once, no more," said Jack. She tightened her lips, leaned over the table, and hissed at the trickster. "Get your ass out of here, now, you are not going to ruin our meal on this opening day."

"That goes for me too," chimed Sugar Dee.

"No harm done, much done with little fun," the trickster shouted. His voice bounced down the stairs and outside to the audience.

"Get the fuck out," she hissed and clenched her teeth. The arteries on her neck and hands beat a wild malison.

"Mister Griever, please leave now," mewled Sugar Dee.

"Fair maidens," the trickster mocked with a simian smile, "the mind monkey has come to liberate thee." He moved closer to Sugar Dee and pointed at the bizarre animals that roamed on her breasts.

Matteo Ricci, meanwhile, thrust his head from the folds of the shoulder pack. The trickster freed the cock on the table and then examined the ornate a la carte menu. When the cock scratched on the white linen, the two women screamed and abandoned their chairs.

"Foul cock," screamed Jack.

"Nouvelle cuisine, artichoke and palm hearts, escargot, cheese flan, chicken liver mousse, pheasant liver paté, capers and onions, white wine sauce, tomato sauce and beef marrow, lobster sauce and cayenne pepper, olive oil and basil, sorrel over salmon, scallops, sole, mussels, trout, turbot, and wild duck, boned quail with truffles, marinated saddle of venison, sausage, pink lamb, veal, and custards, pancakes, persimmon, sponge cakes, poached pears with chocolate sauce, watermelon, but no *lamproie à la bordelaise*," the trickster chanted behind the table. He tore the pages from the menu and folded them four times.

"Where was that on the menu?"

"Pierre told me to improvise, imagine an edible menu," he said and launched the first plane, which banked to the right and crashed in a luminous ocean on the window. The second plane soared back to the dark bar, and the third double-looped and stormed the hors d'oeuvres on a table where two cadres and a foreign banker were seated.

"*Hors de combat*," said the banker, trained to praise the moment until the check arrives. He smiled and parked the paper plane on a vacant chair.

Sammie Moon, seated on the other side of the dining room with her back to the trickster, was captivated by the impeccable blond and did not notice the commotion over the cock and paper planes. She turned too late; the trickster had doubled his pace down the spiral stairs.

The fourth plane crashed on launch into the chest of a doorman who invited the trickster to leave the restaurant. The waiters, the hat check woman, and the doormen surrounded the trickster at the table. The cock spread his wings, sickle feathers shivered, and he crapped on a starched napkin. The waiter in a crisp white apron smiled; the others snickered. The hatchecker covered her mouth with her hands to hold back a burst of laughter.

"Sir, you go now."

"Why?"

"You must go outside."

"The cock, right?"

"No, not cock."

"My opera clothes, then?"

"No, not coat."

"What then?"

"No necktie," chanted the doormen.

"What?"

"No necktie, no eat."

"Who would believe this?"

"Sir, must wear necktie," said the hatchecker.

"Good riddance," shouted Jack.

"Good, good riddance," chimed Sugar Dee.

"The revolution for a necktie," said the trickster with a flourish. He punched his ear with his thumb, gathered his cock under his arm, and hooted down the stairs to the entrance. There, he raised the cock high, and the audience applauded his wild performance.

The Peking Hotel, about two miles from the restaurant, was one of the few places to hire a taxicab. Griever told the dispatcher that his destination was the Customs and Securities Bureau, showed him the address on the letter he had received, and waited for a driver.

"Mister de Hocus," the cadre announced from behind a high counter at the Customs Bureau. He repeated the name twice more, varied his pronunciation, until the trickster responded.

"De Hocus here."

"Mister de Hocus," the cadre whispered over the counter.

"Here."

"Please, what is ultralight?"

"Serious?"

"What, cigarettes?"

"No, no," the trickster laughed.

"What, weapons?"

"No, no," soughed the trickster, "ultralights are aluminum tubed recreational airplanes powered, in this case, with snowmobile engines."

"Yes, we understand," the cadre said. He leaned over a book opened to a section on airplanes. His hair, trimmed too short, bristled like a swine, and his mouth seemed to unfold when he raised his voice. He fingered a paragraph on the Flying Tigers.

"Flying Roosters?" the trickster teased as he leaned over and watched the cadre move his hand over the pictures.

"You pay, we give you airplanes," he shouted.

"These Patronia Microlights are for hire," the trickster said. He tried to loosen the draconic customs regulations with humor. "Listen, we can shoot down a few capitalists for price, joint ventures, part of the new responsibilities market reforms, how about that for a deal?"

"Two thousand dollars."

"What?"

"One thousand each airplane, no checks."

"How many?"

"Two crates, two thousand, cash," said the cadre.

"No shit," said the trickster.

"You pay now."

"With what?"

"You, come back with cash," said the cadre. He punched the ultralight pictures and smiled; he waved his hands, and closed the thick airplane book. Then he closed the window over the counter and locked the file cabinets.

Outside, the trickster rolled over on his back in the brittle weeds and painted the faces of several friends bunched together on a train. Slyboots Browne, the mixedblood who built Patronia Microlights in a barn on the White Earth Reservation in Minnesota, shipped two ultralights to the trickster; he hoped the cadres would be impressed and order millions of airplanes.

Griever mused that one ultralight would be enough

207

when he remembered that Slyboots, who was a graduate of Dartmouth College, intended one to bribe the cadres to release the second airplane. The trickster leaped back to the customs bureau, and with a popular fashion magazine, he persuaded a woman to reveal where the cadre had gone for lunch.

The Red Guards closed thousands of restaurants in the nation during the Cultural Revolution. The Phoenix, however, located on Donghuan Road near the Friendship Store and Ritan Park, survived the purge, not because it was one of the best restaurants, but because high cadres gathered there to drink and tell stories about the barbarians.

Griever leaned back on his heels, tapped the toes of his shoes together at the threshold, and twisted a wild hair on his temple. He marched through the entrance and came down in the thick smoke and humid shadows near the kitchen; when the curtains parted, harried women appeared in billows of steam with cracked platters of dark meat, broken vegetables, and pure white rice. The trickster imagined sweet and sour mongrel, or rat steaks, and his nose closed on the smell. When the government ordered the removal of canine pets, thousands of animals, dead and alive, were sold to restaurants. Fatted dog stew and glutinous rice dog soup were favored dishes in earlier times, as were ravens, swallows, and owls. Dog meat, on the other hand, was not recommended with distilled spirits because it could induce hemorrhoids. Small pain for the consumption of a devoted pet.

Griever roamed between the dark booths in search of the cadre from the Customs and Securities Bureau. The concrete floor was stained with sauce and spit; chicken and animal bones were brushed to the floor at the end of the tables. Overhead, demonic webs bound the cracks in the plaster and trailed down the mold stained walls behind the booths at the back of the restaurant.

208

"Gloome," shouted the trickster, "smack me cold, what in the name of civilization are you doing here?" He was pleased to find a familiar face, even Colin Gloome.

"Celebrating," he mumbled and raised a bottle. "That coat, who is your tailor?" He smiled and then laughed, a rare moment.

"Celebrating what?"

"Plastic surgery," he responded in slow motions, "tomorrow, this will be gone for good, and this, and this, tucks, forehead lifts, chemical peels, even a dermabrasion." Gloome pinched the loose skin under his chin, and his cheeks.

"What is a dermabrasion?"

"Listen," he whispered and then remained silent.

"Gloome, hang onto your cock tomorrow," said the trickster, "and watch out for the dog meat, it causes hemorrhoids."

"Dogs, what brings you here?"

"Communist bribes."

"For what?"

"Ultralights."

"Right," he mumbled and waved at the two unshaven cadres in the booth, "and for the right price these two commies found me a plastic surgeon."

"Keep your chin up," said the trickster. He punched his ear and moved down the aisle. Small bones crunched at the end of each table.

Five tables back on the right, the customs cadre turned in the booth and covered his face with a menu to avoid the trickster, but his moves were too obvious. The other cadres in the booth were troubled that their meal and their ideological privities had been interrupted by a barbarian in borrowed opera clothes.

"Listen, about the ultralights," said the trickster. He tilted his head to the right, leaned closer to examine their meals and pointed with two fingers. "What's that, rat or dog?"

"You, come back later," the customs cadre said a second time with a frown. He handed the trickster a menu, tattered and stained, and the other cadres mumbled and waved at him to leave the booth, to leave the restaurant. "Come back later to customs desk, later you pay."

The trickster agreed, bowed, and then, curious, he circled the booths at the back, behind threadbare curtains where the smoke was thinner and a whisper could be heard. Michael Grusenberg and his wife, Fanya Orluk, were seated, backs to the moist wall, with two high cadres who wore dark suits and silk neckties. The trickster crunched their bones and leaned into their booth.

"Mister de Hocus, to what do we owe this honor?" Grusenberg was courteous, but his hands remained closed when he listened.

"Private, right?"

"Perhaps we could talk at another time," he said with a polite smile. His closed hands loomed on the table. The cadre in the corner leaned forward, focused his camera, and shot a photograph of the trickster.

"Commie asshole," shouted the trickster, blinded from the flash, "give me that camera." He blinked several times and then leaped on the table; he broke plates, toppled beer bottles, and pursued the cadre. "Commie cocksucker spies," he roared and reached for the cadre who cowered in the corner of the booth.

Matteo Ricci crowed undercover.

The trickster walked on the cadre, kneed his narrow chest, threw open the back of the camera, unrolled and exposed the film. Seconds later, several tattooed men from the kitchen raised the trickster on their shoulders, carried him through the restaurant and heaved him into the street.

"No foreign dogs allowed," said one man; his thick

apron was stained with blood and barbules. His short muscular arms tolled at his sides, and at the same time he spat at the side of the trickster.

Griever met the customs cadre later in the afternoon and traded one ultralight for the other with a promise that he would provide flight instruction. The cadre authorized a triune seal, three official scarlet chops. One to possess the ultralight, the second to transport the crate on the streets, and the third to load the crate on the train.

¶ Blue Bones

The Marxmass Carnival, a secular crotch where class wars and solemn communions contend, was ordained by Sister Eternal Flame, a mixedblood who renounced the cloister to establish a scapehouse for wounded women. She warned that the "costume mass must be held under a whole moon, a natural and wild endeavor."

Flame observed the prime carnival when she returned to the reservation and turned her considerable passions to celebrate with lost and lonesome women. Last year she conducted three carnivals because no one could agree on the same moon.

Griever, who danced at the reservation carnivals, marked the observance on the same night the nation celebrated the autumn moon festival. The low moon burst on the pond and auras washed between the weeds. Bats dropped from seams in the eaves and wheeled behind the plane trees.

Egas Zhang hindered the plan to hold the carnival in the guest house; he warned that a dance would raise too much dust, which would cover the dishes in the dining room. The teachers were amused over his duteous pose; he had never been concerned about coal and lime dust, or the toxic chemicals in the air and water.

An agreement was reached when he was invited to broker the purchase of beer, cold cuisine, and a selection of

212

moon cakes, at four times the normal cost. The beer was clouded and thick, and the apples he provided were bruised from the bottom of the baskets. The moon cakes, however, were handsome, a splendid selection in the shape of fish and various animals; some were decorated with the image of a rabbit under a cassia tree and filled with melon seeds, almonds, orange peel, meats, and cassia blossoms.

The rabbit moon cakes were in the center of the largest table, enclosed in a great wall of pomegranates, bruised apples, and small hard medicinal pears.

Griever was on the terrace behind the guest house; he was alone that afternoon, working on his ultralight, when the beer, moon cakes, and coal, much to his surprise, were delivered at the same time. For months no one had used the terrace on the pond, a suitable place to assemble his airplane with no interruptions. The trickster opened the crate and organized the parts in even rows on the concrete; nylon flight surfaces spread on the upper tier; aluminum supports, bucket seat, foot controls, cables, and the small engine on the lower tiers. The instructions were written in four languages; the numbers and illustrations seemed clear, but not much more.

The two men who delivered the moon cakes, modern men on a motor scooter, scorned the man who pushed a handcart loaded with coal. Their voices whined and chattered over the coal man while he shoveled his load onto a pile behind the guest house. The trickster conceded their tone of voice, but he misconstrued their derision of the coal man as technological elitism. The wind moved the coal dust down the tiers to the pond; the seams in the concrete and the sand near shore were black.

"Pardon me," said the coal man from behind his handcart, "what is that you have there?" The men at the window were troubled; they sneered at the coal man and the teacher.

213

"Ultralight airplane."

"News to me," he seemed to whisper at an enormous distance from the terrace. His head was shaved and he wore white plastic mittens which he never removed, not even to wipe his nose. The gloves and his even white teeth were in wild contrast to his face, loose clothes, and cloth coolie shoes, which were black with coal dust, so black that he seemed to hide the late slant of the sun and the shimmer on the dead water.

"Griever is my name," he said and reached to shake hands with the coal man, who did not remove his plastic mittens.

"Lindbergh," he whispered.

"Marxmass Carnival?"

"What was that?"

"Wild mittens," said the trickster who had not heard the name and continued to make conversation while he identified parts in the instructions.

"Present from my mother," he said and wiped his swollen nose, "she would protect the hands of an artist sentenced to push a coal cart."

"Painter?"

"Yes, nudes," he said and smiled.

"Right, and this is your reeducation," the trickster said and bolted two aluminum braces to the main structure of the ultralight.

"Coal dust," he sighed, "better than lime."

"What did you do to deserve this?"

"Painted an abstract series on cunts, breasts, and bound feet," he said and outlined with his hands the shapes on the canvas.

"Those old cadres must have loved a bound foot," said the trickster. He moved one tier closer to the coal man and fastened two cables from the wings to the triangle wheel braces.

214

"The cadres were moved by the withered feet, but told me to eliminate the bourgeois breasts and cunts," said the coal man, "or be sentenced to a labor reform camp."

"From tits to coal."

"Lime first, for nine months," he said and turned his head to the side, "and then coal, but there was more to it than a simple cunt."

"Golden lilies for the cadres," the trickster shouted, and his voice was heard by people on the road around the pond. The two men at the window did not understand.

"The cadres praised my revisions," said the coal man, "but when I pointed out that the bound feet were diseased and the gangrene on the arch represented the corruption in our government, the cadres condemned me to five years' public labor, the last two in lime and coal."

"Wait a minute," said the trickster. He moved closer to the coal man, then touched and rubbed the dust on his cheek. "What are you, mixedblood?"

"American," he said and wiped his nose.

"Where were you born?"

"Tianjin, on the same day Charles Lindbergh flew over the Arctic Circle and landed in China," he said, laughed, and lowered his head to continue. "My father was from Washington, but he disappeared, 'duck death' the cadres claim, and I was educated at the multiracial mission school here."

"Marvelous, can you fly."

"No, no, never have, can you?"

"No, but the instructions seem complete enough," said the trickster. He wheeled his hands over the three tiers of parts. "Say, how about being my guest at the carnival tonight?"

"Not possible," he said and moved his cart.

"Why not?"

"We are not allowed to leave the dormitories."

"Where are the dormitories?"

"Old Matsushima Road."

"Can we do anything, an ultralight escape?"

"Not tonight," he whispered and pushed the cart down the road past the pond to the coal depot where he loaded and unloaded seven more times before dark.

Griever followed the instructions, tightened the cables, mounted the seat and engine, and then at dusk, when the coal man was behind his last load, he called the teachers down to the terrace and started the engine. The propeller shuddered and bounced back several times. The trickster tuned the engine and roared down the road, turned around the pond, and over the bridge, but he did not leave the ground that night in his ultralight.

The moon leaned over the pond, wavered, separated with the breeze, and then flooded the dining room. The whistle of a distant steam engine and the strident voice from an opera on television combined in the moist corners and creases of the guest house.

Gingerie Anderson-Peterson was the first to arrive at the carnival; too eager, she nibbled on the inside of her cheek in the dark dining room. She wore a hot pink hobble skirt with a loose lace bodice that revealed her nipples in the best light, and she carried a mask decorated with chicken feathers. The moon spread her shadow over the concrete floor; she danced from window to window, waved the mask at her image on the small panes, and then ducked behind the curtains.

Carnegie Morgan pushed open the double doors, threw the light switches, shattered the silence. He had painted his lips and fingernails blood red and wore a blond wig, blue velvet gown, pearls, and silver high heeled shoes. Unaware that he was not alone, he cakewalked around the tables, touched the moon cakes, whispered the names of women— diminutives, and confessed his sexual fantasies over the pears. He licked his fingers, connected the stereo cables to the speakers, and selected music taped on cassettes. He started with acid rock and increased the volume ten decibels a turn, louder and louder until the windows rattled; then he cut the sound and listened to his ears burn in the silence.

"Miss Gingerie, you wear her clothes."

"Egas, darling, you noticed."

"Chinese people not allowed to hear such music," Egas shouted from the double doors, prepared to be heard over the amplified sound. "Too much music in dining room cause windows to break and chairs lose glue."

"Egas, you are a smart man, never use opium man," he said from behind the table of moon cakes. Morgan mounted earphones and turned the volume higher; the sound from his head was audible clear across the dining room.

Gingerie moved down the inside wall, through the double doors and the entrance hall, to the outside. She circled the pond and returned to the terrace. She waited there on the lowest tier, removed her red shoes and black lace stockings, and soaked her feet. Small carp nibbled on her fat toes in the dead water. Behind her, the other teachers gathered in the dining room. She listened to their carnival voices; the music was too loud to hear whether her name was spoken. The open windows rattled, the moon shivered on the pond. She whispered to the carp how much she loved romantic music and hated loud rock; she wanted to be missed.

The African students assembled on the terrace, uncertain about the invitation to the carnival, and watched the teachers through the windows.

Hannah Dustan paraded inside as an empress dowager; she wore a peculiar headdress, high collar, loose gown, and a brocaded cloak. Two women from her computer course stood at her side dressed in tailored wool business suits.

The ostentatious reversal appeared less bizarre than she had intended; one student held a wide red umbrella over the dowager as she flounced around the moon cakes.

Colin Gloome hobbled through the double doors, his head and neck sealed with bandages, the most unusual carnival costume. He stood in the center of the room and waited to be recognized.

"Gloome, when can we see the new you?"

"Carnegie, you look good in drag, smashing dress, reminds me of my high school graduation," he said with uncommon complaisance, "would the man in blue like to dance?"

"No shit," said Carnie with his hands held high, "who would believe that a simple tuck turned gloom and doom to humor?" He snapped his fingers and thrust his pelvis in time with the high tech pulsation of acid rock.

Griever was outside on the terrace. He had been there for more than an hour before he was recognized behind his color and costume. He wiped his nose at the window and watched the teachers dance.

Gingerie and the African students did not see the trickster at the windows, but Sugar Dee, who was pursued by more than a dozen Algerian watchmakers, noticed his disguise and screamed the name of the trickster twice, three times, before she was heard over the music. "The black one, there, there, at the window, the one with the black face," she said and pointed, but the trickster had moved back from the windows.

"Africans, sweetie," said the dowager.

"Griever, he was blacker," she insisted.

"Call me Lindbergh," said the trickster. He leaped through the window, a minstrel, into the dining room where he turned and summoned the others to come in from the terrace; he waited, smiled at the dowager, danced around her ladies, and then when no one followed him, he stepped back out the window to the terrace. He was dressed in loose black clothes, cloth coolie shoes, and white plastic mittens; his face, neck, and ankles were blackened with coal dust.

"Grievah, yah look terrible," said Gingerie.

"Never mind the face, my darling, these are vernal hands," said the trickster. He reached for her thighs, pulled her down the tiers, closer to the pond, and massaged her breasts.

"Venal, yah mean."

"Your bare feet are beautiful in the light of the moon," the trickster whispered close to her ear. "Your breasts are succulent."

"Fat feet," she whispered.

"Big tits."

"Grievah, stop that now."

"One breast then," he said and lowered the lace bodice. He balanced one plump breast on a plastic mitten and sucked the enormous black nipple.

Egas Zhang, meanwhile, was driven past his narrow tolerance for unreined behavior and decadent rock music. Sounds from the wild carnival reached the dormitories; students gathered outside to watch and mimic dance moves. Egas, the petit despot, shamed the students and warned the teachers several times to lower the volume and close the curtains. When the noise increased, he cut the electrical power to the dining room. The teachers and visitors stood mute in the shadows and then moved the carnival to the terrace on the pond.

The African students danced with the Algerian watchmakers to rock music from a small portable tape recorder. Gloome danced with the dowager, Carnegie pursued Sugar Dee and Jack, Gingerie moved from the trickster to Luther Holes, who appeared late dressed like a diocesan priest.

Egas, on the other hand, walked back to the dormitories with Faith, the student monitor.

Kangmei, shrouded in her burnoose, arrived on her prairie schooner with Wu Chou and the others from Obo Island. She reined the horse near a tree and moved in the shadows. Shitou, the stone shaman, wore bear claws and small mirrors that held the moon. Sandie and Pigsie wore basketball uniforms and dribbled a ball through the coal dust on the terrace. Yaba Gezi, the mute pigeon, moved in blue light; he held an escape distance on the shore of the pond. Wu Chou, the warrior clown and keeper of the campus gate, was dressed in his finest opera costume; he smiled and touched each teacher and student with pleasure.

"Where is Hester Hua Dan?" asked Griever.

"No one has seen her," said the warrior clown. "She came through the gate late last night, worried and tormented, but she was not there at the usual time this morning."

"Where is Matsushima Road?"

"The old road?"

"Yes," said the trickster, "do you know how to get there, where the labor reform dormitories are located?" He wiped his nose with the plastic mitten.

"*Laogai* dormitories," said Wu Chou.

"What does that mean?"

"Reform through labor," mocked the warrior clown.

"Come with me now."

"Where?"

"To the *laogai* with moon cakes," said the trickster and pushed the warrior clown to the prairie schooner. He had loaded the best moon cakes into two cloth bundles.

"Have you ever been there?" asked Wu Chou.

"Lindbergh is there."

"Which one?"

"The one with the coal cart."

"So, you borrowed his mittens for the carnival," said the warrior clown, "but no one believed you were a coal hauler."

"Why not?"

"You move like a mind monkey, a clown with coal dust," the warrior clown explained, "not like a man who has listened to the cold, or a man who counts the words in lectures on socialist ideologies to hold his memories together."

Kangmei whistled and the horse pranced past the campus gate, turned down the moat road, and then to the right. The reform dormitories were built close to the old concession road; the small windows were barred, and there were uniformed sentries at the main gate. The trickster punched his ear with a plastic mitten and paced around the schooner in silence. The warrior clown waited on the bench for the mind monkey to reveal his scheme to deliver moon cakes. The trickster leaped, startled the horse, and clapped his plastic mittens together.

"This is it," he commanded and climbed back on the schooner. "We move right up to the main gate and let me do the rest." The horse reared and then trotted with his ears back.

"What is the rest?"

"Follow me, listen, and translate the stories from there," said the trickster. He wiped his nose; his cheeks were marbled with mucus, an allergic reaction to coal dust.

The trickster leaped from the schooner, rushed toward the sentries with his white mittens raised, and rattled the gates. "We have moon cakes for the mixedbloods, moon cakes, free the mixedbloods, moon cakes, moon cakes," the trickster chanted. The sentries raised their weapons.

Wu Chou bowed, smiled, turned his head to the side and told the sentries that he would translate. He said that at a new moon opera rehearsal the teacher and movie actor became "Wu Gang, and when the Jade Emperor ruled that he would be free if he felled a cassia tree, the actor, an invited guest to our country, and one who respects our culture and traditions, pretended to cut a tree, which caused a stack of loose bricks to tumble down on his head."

"My daughter, there, behind the horse, was crossing the moat on the campus, alone on her cart, when a wheel came loose," the trickster intoned and waved his white mittens. "The horse reared and she was thrown into the moat."

"This movie actor, here with his hands in bandages, was buried under coal and bricks," the warrior clown pretended to translate, "and the man who saved him was a humble coal hauler who lives in the labor dormitories."

Kangmei snickered behind her burnoose while the sentries holstered their weapons; one turned to the other; both seemed to recognize the man in the stories.

"Anne Spencer Morrow demands the freedom of the artist, free the coal man," the trickster shouted at the gate. He moved closer to the sentries, smiled, and wiped his nose with a mitten. "Listen, Lindbergh came by and saved my only daughter from a horrible death in the moat. He risked his ass, and now we want to thank him with some moon cakes."

"Well, this coal man saved the movie actor, he threw the bricks right and left, and now, the actor would like to thank the humble coal hauler with moon cakes. The actor believes that he must see the coal man once under the whole moon, as the Jade Emperor told Wu Gang in the new moon opera."

"Li-da-bah," said the sentries.

"Lindbergh, yes, that was his name," said the warrior clown. "Please, the actor owes his soul to this Li-da-bah."

"Li-da-bah," the sentries smiled.

"Moon cakes for the coal man," chanted the trickster.

"Li-da-bah," the sentries laughed.

"Moon cakes for the sentries," chanted the warrior clown. He laughed with them, opened the bundle and presented a choice selection of moon cakes. "Li-da-bah would like moon cakes too, he is a proud worker who does not seek recognition."

"Li-da-bah," the sentries laughed once more. They ate the moon cakes but never responded to the stories the warrior clown told them at the gate.

Griever punched his ear and led the horse and schooner down the dark road to the corner. There, he shouldered the last bundle of moon cakes, turned back with the warrior clown to the dormitories, and peeked through the high, barred window in search of the coal man.

Lindbergh was alone in a room close to the main gate and the sentries. Each brick in the room was a miniature painting, scenes with men and women at work, socialist realism, but the sensuous visage in each scene revealed the loneliness and courage of the painter. He pared his toenails and saved each sliver.

"Lindbergh, over here," the trickster whispered.

"Where, where?"

"Griever with the ultralight," he said with one marbled cheek pressed to the bars. "Listen, we brought the carnival to you, here are some moon cakes." He passed them between the bars, rabbit images and other animals.

"No more, please," he said and returned several to the trickster. "Who would believe that someone threw these into my room?"

"Right, there will be more in small bundles on the terrace near the coal pile," the trickster promised. "Does the moon get in there?"

"Thirteen minutes in the winter."

"Lindbergh what?"

"Wang," he whispered and ate a rabbit moon cake.

223

"Li-da-bah Wang," the trickster mocked. "Mister Wang, tell me, where are the mixedblood tits and cunts in those brick paintings there?"

"The bricks are turned," said the coal man and smiled. His face was clean, but black seams marked his cheeks and forehead; his hands were small white blossoms at the bottom of his dark arms, lilies folded over his narrow chest. "Please, you could spare me much trouble at our reform classes if you would drop moon cakes in all the cells on the row."

"Listen," the trickster boasted, "take these white mittens, you might need another pair to wear before you retire from the coal business."

Kangmei whistled, and the horse clapped back toward the campus. She loosened the reins and told several stories about her real father, stories about his childhood and labor reform, stories that she imagined—concise, vivid, mettlesome stories.

Yaba Gezi was at the campus gate when they returned; he circled with a wild message. Kangmei pulled him on the schooner, and he whispered in her ear, touched her hands, and with two fingers he seemed to write on her cheek.

"What did he say?" asked Griever.

"Someone has fallen into the pond," she translated and slapped the horse with the reins. "He said the water holds a blue light."

"What blue light?"

"Blue stone."

"Shitou is in the pond," shouted the trickster. He leaped from the schooner and ran to the terrace. The teachers and students waited in silence, a *tableau vivant,* on the tiers; the stone man waded in the moon and the deep blue light moved at the bottom of the pond.

Yaba Gezi would dive under the dead water and search for the light, but the stone man shuddered and said the pond should be drained. Sandie and Pigsie rushed around the pond and opened the five valves. The thick water roared like a demon from the huge sewer pipes and flooded the moat. The teachers waited and watched the water leave the last tier, wash over the stones, broken dishes, a fork and two spoons. The moon pillar on the water wavered, seared on both ends where the water drained.

Shitou waded closer to the blue light which was located in a deep trench near the terrace. The light became clearer as the water drained. His smooth shoulders rolled, and the small mirrors on his arms and waist flashed the whole moon in wild dimensions. The teachers were silent, no one moaned, whispered, or even snapped an elbow. The blue light was a court to a secret place, a shared dream that carries voices over a cataract. The dread was intense; the water drained lower and the stone man waded closer to the light at the bottom of the pond.

Shitou raised the bones of babies from the blue muck. He washed the bones, five small heads, and placed them on the tiers; others fitted the little bones to the shapes of bodies on the terrace. The dead water had been a burial place, a killing pond, for unwanted children. Then the stone man touched the blue light, a jade rabbit on a chain tied tight around the neck of a woman.

"Hester Hua Dan," whispered the stone shaman.

"No, no, she has our child," Griever screamed from the lowest tier. "We had a name, a real name." He sloshed through the muck and shallow water; he loosened the blue stone rabbit, washed her hair back, raised her face to the moon, touched the scar, and kissed her bloated cheeks.

The police were not prepared to manage a corpse, foreign teachers in peculiar costumes, shamans with moon mirrors, black men, watchmakers, bare breasted women, hundreds of fish splashing in the mud and shallow water, and the blue bones of babies.

Hester Hua Dan was carried to the terrace where the stone man and the trickster covered her with a brocaded cloak, a feathered mask, silver shoes, and moon cakes.

The police ordered the students back to their dormitories, closed the drains in the pond, and pitched the blue bones back into the cold dead water.

♌ Blue Chicken

Hua Lian, the last to arrive at the carnival, waited in the back of the prairie schooner with the stone man. She appeared on the terrace, dressed in a scarlet silk coat with faces of monkeys embroidered on the collar and sleeves; too late, the dance had ended; solemn teachers had returned to the guest house.

Kangmei, Shitou, Sandie, Pigsie, Yaba Gezi, Li Wen, and the trickster crowded under the sailcloth in the back of the schooner. Hua Lian lighted a small blue lantern and told stories about the moon rabbit to honor the children and Hester Hua Dan.

"The same moon that rises over the ocean lands in the tea water," she said and handed the lantern to the trickster. "The wind that cools the waters scatters the moons like rabbits on a meadow.

"See, the shaman bears come down from the mountains to dream in the gardens," she chanted an orison with her hands over her head. "One bear was alone and hungry, so she said, and the otter brought her seven fishes, and a raven his carrion, but then a rabbit leaped from the brush and told the bear that he had little more than his own body to offer as food. 'Feed on my flesh,' the rabbit told the bear, and then the rabbit saw some magic coals that burned without smoke. . . ."

227

"Hua Lian," the trickster shouted, "your other eye."

"Not now," moaned Pigsie.

"Near the panic holes," said Hua Lian.

"One is darker."

"Not much."

"What happened to the rabbit?"

"The rabbit leaped right into the fire," whispered Hua Lian. "The shaman bear praised the sacrifice, turned the rabbit into the moon, and named the jade rabbit the Moon with Short Front Paws."

"No shit," said the trickster.

"No shit," replied Hua Lian, "and the jade rabbit lived in the moon palace with an immortal who looked like you, a monkey, a trickster teacher."

"Monkey, monkey," chanted Pigsie.

"The revolution ended that jade rabbit monkey shit," the trickster shouted and pushed a wad of paper into his ear to mock the ear readers. "Wu Gang was immortal but, one wild *but*, he wanted to be whole, so he was told to cut down a cassia tree for his freedom, but, one more wild *but*, he was doomed, he might as well have bawled at the moon like the rest of us here, the blows were futile, the tree healed faster than he could cut."

Griever passed the lantern to the stone man and lurched out the back of the schooner. He sloshed below the terrace, routed a panic hole in the blue muck and screamed, smashed his head down, and screamed deeper in the earth.

China opened in pale blue smoke on the night he arrived and closed now in dead water. The trickster crouched at the window in his apartment, a secure corner in the cold concrete. There, he was severed from his shadow in a culture that pretended to understand the monkey king and trickeries; he watched tired faces on the moon, scars, crosses, blue bones, rise over the brick wall and vanish behind the broad leaves.

Griever rolled his nose and cheeks on the walls from one end of the room to the other; his mock silhouette thinned and dissolved near the bathroom. He showered in cold water, changed his shirt, trousers, and shoes, and then heaved the rest of his clothes, books, stones, mementoes over the balcony.

Matteo Ricci crowed on the rail.

The guest house entrance was locked, as usual; the trickster climbed outside through an open window in the dining room. He tied the ultralight airplane to the top of the prairie schooner. The wide cloth wings moved like a moth in the pale light.

Kangmei whistled; the horse shivered and moved around the guest house. The last bats circled the pond and returned to their seams in the eaves. The trickster waved to the warrior clown at the campus gate; he looked back once as the schooner crossed the dead water in the moat.

Matteo Ricci crowed at the corner.

Shitou roused his visual memories and prepared a detailed map of the cities and mountains between Obo Island and Macao. The trickster estimated the distance for each gallon of gasoline, the ultralight held less than three, and marked the nearest cities on the map, places where he could fill the portable tank.

Matteo Ricci crowed from behind the seat of the airplane as it bounced on three wheels over the rough swine earth on the island, lifted and cleared the moat. The trickster circled the willow trees and waved one last time to the stone man and the swine islanders.

"Tell me now, right now," the trickster said in her ear as the ultralight soared over the water park, "what is the secret on that manuscript?"

Kangmei was perched on the bucket seat in front of the

trickster, between his legs. The sacred manuscript her father had given her was tied behind the cock and under the
wing of the airplane. She leaned her head back, loosened
her blond hair on the wind, and told the trickster, over the
roar of the engine, that the secret was a recipe.

"Come now, tell me the truth."

"Would you turn back?"

"Never, not even for a sacred recipe."

"Blue chicken," she shouted.

"What?"

"The recipe is for blue chicken, made with mountain
blue corn and pressed blueberries." She wrapped her arms
around his thighs when the ultralight lost altitude in a
downwind and banked to the right.

"The bear shamans eat blue corn?"

"Blue mountain corn."

"Macao, here we come," the trickster shouted over his
shoulder to Matteo Ricci. He touched the jade rabbit
around his neck and punched his ear twice, three times to
be sure. The cock crowed and pecked at the tether on his
feathered shanks.

❡ Ultralight Escape

Dear China:

The sunrise was sweet and blue, as blue as the meadows on the reservation, and the sun was a courteous child perched on the trees when we circled over Tai Shan Mountain. The ultralight engine is too loud but the mountain and the view over the Temple of Confucius is marvelous.

People stop on narrow paths and wave, we must look like tourists on a bus in the air, and once we scared some peasants when we landed to ask for directions. The real joke is that people never ask directions over here, this is not a map place where people remember an abstract location. We are the map people, not them. We were lost and asked them to make a map in their heads to tell us where they were so we could find out where we were. They know where they are, but we are in the air.

Anyway, the peasants are terrific, places the cadres never allowed us to visit. The old women had no teeth, but no one held back a smile for any reason, not maps or cadres. The children swarmed me, convinced, no doubt, that I was their treasure, an immortal monkey king.

We camped under the wing near Jinan the first night and now we're at Boxian in Anhui Province, somewhere on the map, about four days' flying time, if the weather holds, from our freedom in the old colony at Macao.

231

I never flew an ultralight before, never flew anything, and never knew about laminar flow, stagnation, angle of attack in the air, lift, drag, thrust, until we almost crashed into a moat the first morning we took off from Obo Island in Tianjin. I read the instructions, you can be sure, but forgot to figure that a weight increase would decrease the air speed. Listen to me, I sound like a pilot with less than two hundred pounds of aluminum and a snowmobile engine. We were lucky, a breeze raised the wings at the end of the basketball court, at the last second, otherwise we might have stalled over the moat.

The ultralight carries less than three gallons of gas which takes us about two hundred miles. We estimate the distance with care because there are no instruments. The Patronia Microlight soars like a crow, and tell your brother Slyboots this is the place for ultralights, the peasants are on the road with cash in hand.

I have a feel of the air now, and this view of the nation, this world of peasants, is very peaceful, like those brush strokes in an ink painting. Those artists must have been flying in their heads, but not with the roar of an engine. Now, for the first time, I can see from the air what they must have seen to paint their pictures.

We even saw some wandering lights at dawn, but nothing like that gigantic flying object that a pilot saw over the western provinces. More people see lights over here than anywhere else in the world. This is a nation of peasants who live in the sky in the dark.

The Marxmass Carnival was horrible this year, no more carnivals like that for me. No panic holes are deep enough to hold my rage over what happened that night.

Remember Egas Zhang?

The director of the foreign affairs bureau?

Well, that evil bastard drowned Hester Hua Dan and Kuan Yin, her beautiful daughter with the same name as the bodhisattva who captured the mind monkey for the Jade Emperor in one of those stories from *The Journey to the West*, the book you sent to me. He drowned his own child and granddaughter in the pond behind the guest house.

Egas was always asking me for aphrodisiacs, bear paws and gallbladders. If I ever see him again he'll be walking and talking like a mutant hermaphrodite, because I gave him a strong dose of estrogen. The dust he thinks is bear paw will give him the big tits he always wanted to see, his very own tits, and raise his voice in less than a week.

Evil and death surrounded that concrete place, soon the bats will leave the guest house for the mountains. Shitou, the old stone man, said "Drown a girl, give birth to a monster," when we carried Hester Hua Dan from the pond.

No more panic holes for me because the air has become the place to release my rage. I roar at the dawn, I roar at the wind, I roar at nothing and everything seems fine now, I am in my own painting over the mountains. So far, the ultralight engine has been louder than my voice. Do you suppose people hear me on the ground?

Kangmei and Matteo Ricci are with me. She's a mixedblood, related to Hester Hua Dan and Kuan Yin. You can imagine what the peasants must think when we come down out of the air, a mixedblood barbarian trickster in an opera coat, a mixedblood blonde who speaks Chinese, wears a cape with bundles of silk seeds under her arms, and a cock tied behind the ultralight seat. Kangmei knows how to raise silk worms and where to find wild ginseng, can you imagine silk farmers on the reservation?

So far we haven't had any trouble finding gasoline even though it's rationed and we don't have a card. The Chinese must think we are part of some new airborne monkey

233

opera, everything is a play over here, so we must be the new scene.

Kangmei was born here but her father was an American, he died in a labor camp during the earthquake at Tangshan. She inherited small bones from her mother and blond hair from her father, which was necessary for her flight to freedom, because, if she weighed ten pounds more we might have crashed in the moat, and if she had black hair she might have been arrested. We still have a little difficulty taking off with a full tank of gas. Tomorrow we plan to stop more often and take on less gasoline at one time, unless, of course, we have ten miles of good runway.

Remember those manuscripts I told you about? Well, Kangmei has one that her father gave to her, and guess what it says? Would you believe that those sacred bear scrolls are nothing more than recipes? What else, right? Listen, this manuscript has a marvelous recipe for blue chicken, the cuisine of shaman bears, who, I am told, cultivated the first blue corn in the mountains over here.

Well, here it is dark now, and guess who forgot to bring a flashlight? We even forgot to bring candles, but there's still a generous slice of the moon left tonight. There's a post office in the village down the road, I want to mail this before we hit the air tomorrow at dawn.

I have much to tell you about my experiences here, at the guest house, at Maxim's de Beijing, and hog basketball games at Obo Island, but those stories must wait for another time. For now, let me tell you that I was there at the beginning of the next revolution in this great opera over here, I was at the opening of Maxim's, the ultimate in slow food, on the same day that Mao Zedong declared the People's Republic of China at Tiananmen Square.

Macao is a few more days away, write to me there, or better yet, why not meet us there? Listen, we have some

234

good stories about foot binding too, but as the peasants say, "You can't eat a steamed bun in one bite, and you can't wrap fire in paper." This is a marvelous world of tricksters.

Love,

Griever de Lindbergh

EPILOGUE

My wife Laura Hall and I were teachers for several months
at Tianjin University. We visited Maxim's de Beijing the
day it opened on the thirty-fourth anniversary of the
founding of the People's Republic of China. I was turned
away that morning because I was not wearing a necktie;
however, when I explained that I was there to examine the
interior reproduction and not to eat, the dress code was
overlooked for the moment. The waiters were nervous; the
restaurant smelled of varnish.

Li Rui-Huan, the Mayor of Tianjin, is quoted from his
speech at the National Day dinner sponsored by the Tianjin
Municipal People's Government on September 29, 1983.
References to the foreign concessions map are based on a
tattered copy found at the back of a desk drawer in the
guest house at Tianjin University. The undergraduate language students in my classes responded with silence to the
concession map and the information it contained.

References to the Lazarist Sisters of Saint Vincent de
Paul appeared in *The New Yorker*, May 17, 1982, part two
of a four part article on Tianjin by John Hersey. The adventures of Herbert Hoover are quoted from *The Spirit
Soldiers: A Historical Narrative of the Boxer Rebellion* by
Richard O'Connor. The events in Victoria Park were described in *The Boxer Rising: A History of the Boxer Trou-*

236

ble in China (special articles reprinted from the *Shanghai Mercury*). References to Ernest Hemingway appeared in *American and Chinese Communists, 1927–1945: A Persuading Encounter* by Kenneth E. Shewmaker. The experiences of Mikhail Borodin are discussed in *To Change China: Western Advisers in China 1620–1960* by Jonathan Spence.

The author has made use of information about Zhou Enlai from *Coming of Grace,* an illustrated biography by Ed Hammond. Wei Jingsheng, Fu Yuehua, and others detained in prisons and labor reform camps are quoted from *China: Violations of Human Rights,* published by Amnesty International. References to Alicia Little, president of the Natural Foot Society in China, Lottie Moon, and other missionaries, are found in *Our Ordered Lives Confess* by Irwin T. Hyatt; *The Gospel of Gentility* by Jane Hunter; and chapters seventeen and eighteen in *Barbarians and Mandarins* by Nigel Cameron.

Other publications the author has considered in the imaginative conception of this novel include *The Journey to the West,* translated by Anthony C. Yu; *Monkey,* translated by Arthur Waley; *Chinese Theories of Literature* and *Essentials of Chinese Literary Art* by James J. Y. Liu; *The Chinese Theatre in Modern Times* and *The Performing Arts in Contemporary China* by Colin Mackerras; *The Chinese Language* by John DeFrancis; *Speaking of Chinese* by Raymond Chang and Margaret Scrogin Chang; *Chinese Shadows* by Simon Leys; *Prisoner of Mao* by Bao Ruowang, Jean Pasqualini; *Primitive Revolutionaries in China* by Fei-Ling Davis; *Marxism, Maoism, and Utopianism* by Maurice Meisner; *Foreign Devils on the Silk Road* by Peter Hopkirk; *The Great Chinese Travelers* by Jeannette Mirsky; *The Religions of Mongolia* by Walther Heissig; *The Four Mayor Mysteries of Mainland China* by Paul Dong; *Food in Chinese Culture,* edited by K. C. Chang;

Mao's People by B. Michael Frolic; *Literary Dissent in Communist China* by Merle Goldman.

More recent titles include *China: Alive in the Bitter Sea* by Fox Butterfield; *Son of The Revolution* by Liang Heng and Judith Shapiro; *Six Chapters from My Life "Down-under"* by Yang Jiang; *Long Road Home: China Journal* by Vera Schwarcz; *To Get Rich Is Glorious* by Orville Schell; and articles published in the *New York Times* by Christopher Wren.

Herb Caen, columnist with the *San Francisco Chronicle*, wrote about the first basketball competition between San Francisco and Shanghai, new sister cities, at the same time that President Li Xiannian, People's Republic of China, patted Mickey Mouse on the nose at Disneyland.

"What I miss most is cold drinking water, almost an impossibility to get here without strong political connections," Caen wrote from Beijing. "We piled on the bus and drove to the Great Wall Hotel for hamburgers, American-style, with fries, Coke and catsup. Most of us duck-filled elders just sat and watched the players wolf down at least two hamburgers each. . . .

"I returned from the People's Republic of China repeating the traveler's most important mantra, 'Don't complain, don't compare,' but I guess one is permitted to observe," Caen wrote the next day from Hong Kong. "What one observes, among other things, is that after three-thousand years of civilization and culture, the Chinese still don't know how to run a hotel. . . . Poor China, with all those mouths to feed and bodies to clothe and house. Tourism is probably far down on the socialistic list of priorities, but the Chinese are hungry for foreign exchange."

President Li Xiannian was in the United States to sign an agreement with President Ronald Reagan that allows the People's Republic of China to buy American reactors and other nuclear technology "designed for the peaceful use, and only the peaceful use of nuclear materials."